The Fly-ahead Boy

The Fly-ahead Boy
Geoffrey Riddell

Copyright © 2013 Geoffrey Riddell

ISBN: 978-0-9874978-8-8

Adventure, science fiction, children and young adult

Published by Geoffrey Riddell 1378 Old Tolmie Rd Tolmie 3723
Victoria Australia

A fly-ahead boy pilots a Fly-ahead – his own tiny space ship, that
scouts out ahead of the main ship, to make sure space is safe.
Only a child can fit in the Fly-ahead, because it is very small – to
save fuel, and to be a tiny target in times of danger.

Mark is travelling with his family across space. Out of nothing
their ship starts coming apart, and then, when things get even
worse, everyone is saved, everyone except him, by a large ship
that just happens to be there. Something is not right. He is left
alone in space, to die. His time is running out, the air is turning
poison, but the big ship isn't going to save him – they are using
him as bait, to trap a little scout ship when it answers his distress
beacon. Mark's adventures begin.

The Fly-ahead Boy is the first book in the Alito series.

THE FLY AHEAD BOY

FEAR AND LONGING

He was sick. He was scared. He was tired. Everything kept tumbling slowly over and over – the floor became a wall, the ceiling, then a wall, then the floor again, then rose into being a wall. Dad had come, and said 'You can be in charge little man, while we get a few repairs done up front…arm? <u>There</u> you go, ship's watch and all'.

They waited in the playroom, but nobody came for them. The slide tube hatch wouldn't open. His little sisters kept looking at him, hoping he would fix everything, but he knew he was too small. The only things that had lights on were the emergency signs, and the escape pod chamber.

The ship was making un-natural noises, and moving around. Then they saw red flashing. The distress beacon had been launched.

He helped his sisters get into the pod, then he climbed in too. They could wait safely in here with him. There was a new yucky feeling inside him – being in the emergency pod was very final.

The jettison button started flashing hard orange. So did the matching one back in the playroom. The pod's entry hatch hadn't closed properly.

He couldn't get the lid to shut. It made no difference how hard he tried. His arms were too small. He wasn't strong enough.

He got back out, and shut the lid from the outside. The girls were safe. It was the best he could do.

Starlight stopped coming in the window – a large lump of ship was moving past. Scraping along the hull. Their ship was broken. He was worrying if the pod didn't go now it would get trapped. He shut the chamber end, and pressed the button. He would wait for Mum and Dad to come for him. He felt very brave. I'm five, he thought, and I've done a really brave thing.

Starlight again.

He climbed over the floor, and down a wall, to look out the little round window.

He watched his sisters' pod flashing its way to safety. A big ship had come.

He waited, hoping to see people coming for him in a shuttle, or a service bubble. The pods had a count-down time before they rocketed away to the nearest Safe Satellite. The big ship was collecting them into its cargo dock before that happened.

The view from the window kept changing, as the playroom rolled slowly over and over. He couldn't see the big ship's brightly lit cargo dock any more, or even the flashing pods now. All he could see was stars, and then slowly, as the floor rolled from beneath him, the rest of his family's ship began to fill the window. He watched the main hull section fly to pieces as the liquid gas tanks ruptured. The little tube he was in, the children's area, was by itself, separate, torn off, and carrying him away.

He watched the rescuing ship turn off its floodlights, close its cargo bay, and steadily move off into the darkness, until it was gone. He didn't understand. The beacon would go a different colour to mark the wreck when there was no life left in it. All space was being told he was still here, needing to be rescued. He thought of his Mum's face, her eyes when she looked at him, and his Dad's voice. They wouldn't leave him behind. Something was really really wrong.

ALONE IN THE HUGENESS OF SPACE

Just the steady flash of the distress beacon lighting things in the playroom, from a different angle each time through the little window, and blackness outside. He cried, only a little bit, then he turned on his playvision while he waited, and watched his favourite Planetman.

The colours on the little screen were brighter because the playroom was dark. Blue Skies One was being invaded, and the alien ship was impenetrable, until Planetman snuck up close, and aimed weak rays in from lots of angles to form a heatball inside, so the aliens got hot, and had to come out. He didn't care any more whether Planetman won or lost. He couldn't concentrate, because he kept wondering if anyone was coming back for him. Nobody.

He hugged Dad's watch to his chest.

A big sob came out of him that he wasn't expecting, and then he cried, from the bottom of his heart, with all of him.

The playroom was getting cold. Really cold. He curled himself up small to be warmer.

After a long time, weak light shone across the little round window. Another ship was out there. It would have to hurry. He was gulping like a fish without any water, and he had the most terrible headache he'd ever had in his whole life. The air in the playroom was nearly used up. He tried to look sideways through the window with his face squashed against the glass, but he couldn't see the ship.

The light got even weaker, like they were turning it down. Maybe they were getting ready to leave, or already going away. They probably thought the emergency beacon was faulty because they didn't find him in the ship's wreck. He was here, drifting away in the dark. Drifting, drifting. There was no way to call out help. No way that would ever be heard by anyone.

He put his Planetman doll and the Gorgelzoonies' space-ship toy into the escape pod launcher. He didn't want them trapped inside this icy empty broken piece of home. The playroom was going to roll over and over forever across the Universe. They could fly away to a new adventure. He closed the chamber. Drops of water were running all over him, coming out of his skin, making his fingers slippery as he pressed the buttons. Bad air poisoning. He wouldn't be alive much longer.

Planetman was outside now, tiny and alone in the vastness of space. No-one would see the little figure. Now they both needed rescuing. He wanted Planetman back, so they could die together.

'Sorry Planetman,' he said sadly to himself.

The Gorgelzoony ship had swelled into a broken mess because there was no atmosphere pressure out there. Spreading out in space the brightly coloured pieces looked big. Nearly big enough for someone to see. He opened the chamber again, and put every loose thing in the playroom inside it – the cushions, the teacher's teapot, and all the coloured writers. There was nothing left in the playroom, only himself. He pressed the buttons for the last time.

Nothing happened. He wasn't thinking properly, just standing looking at the things still in there, not out in space. The escape pod launcher had no more power. His thoughts were moving slower and slower through his head, until he realised everything was over, all of his life.

He went back to the little round window, to look out into space while he waited to die. His head came to rest on the window surround. He wanted the company of the night sky one last time. He turned his eyes to the stars, and got a fright. A big head was looking back at him.

RESCUED, SORT OF

It didn't feel very safe, being out in space between his playroom and the man's vessel in only a swollen plastic bubble. It had 'Emergency Rescue – for pet use only' written on it. He had doubts about the little ship that was rescuing him too – it was smaller even than his broken-off playroom bit. He was in it now.

The hatch closed. Things hissed. The plastic bubble went a bit floppy. The man was taking gear off himself, and putting it into slider cupboards in the walls. Now he was unzipping the bubble.

'Am I glad you lot came along. We might draw the Line, but that doesn't stop thumping great cruisers that come from anybody's guess where crossing it... That's it: you have a good breathe now – nothing like fresh air. Quiet little fella, aren't you.'

The man was folding the plastic bubble flat and putting it away. The man had a golden ring on one finger, with a little picture on it.

'Having a look around, hey?... You like this ring? Not my mother, or my girl friend – just a beautiful woman from a long time ago. She keeps me company.'

        'There was a big ship. My family are rescued in a big ship. We have to go to it... <u>Please</u>.'

        'Sorry. That I can't do. For three reasons: they weren't supposed to be here, I was spying on them, and they move a lot, lot faster than me, so we would never catch up.'

'Then you can send them a message, so they know where I am.'

Silence in the little craft. The drive system sounded like his mother's vacuum cleaner, quiet and weak.

'Why not? <u>Why</u> can't you?'

'Because, little man, once they know I've seen them here they will hunt me down. Come on, I need to be in the cockpit keeping a lookout.'

'Then you should have a better motor, for running away.'

He followed the man through a slide tube, into a small cockpit. The man was strapping himself into the seat.

'Why haven't you got a better motor,' he asked accusingly.

He felt angry and unhappy, about everything.

'I do have a better motor, little man, and mine shooters, and decoy tailstreams, but until I figure out what to do with you I can't use any of it... I wonder if I could fit you into the loose rubbish tube.'

The man was reaching around, trying to grab him.

'Hey, stop that. Come on kid... Look, you're being silly, where do you think you're going to run? I can reach every part of this cockpit without unstrapping myself. Yes. Even behind me. Got you, you little varmint. Sorry about this. I'm not trained to handle kids... Look, if they catch us, it's <u>zap</u> – <u>poof</u>, and you and I will be very sick little beings. Cooked and splattered.'

'Why.'

He didn't ask it as a question, because it was a demanding criticism. Everything was all wrong, and this man only seemed to know how to make things worse.

'Because they don't want anyone to know they were here, and they will want to steal this little ship without us alive in it complicating things.'

The man was straining, reaching across, screwing the lid off the loose rubbish tube. This was the second time the man had tried to stuff him into something. First the pet bubble thing, and now this.

'<u>No</u>. I'm <u>not</u> going in head first.'

'Who said you were? I'm just seeing if it would fit.'

'That's not funny. Are you playing with me?'

The man was still strapped into the pilot seat, arms stretched out, holding him up inside the little cabin, in front of the tube. The man stopped to think.

'Yes. I suppose I am. Sorry, your royal grumpiness. Three years I've been up here by myself. You are the most fantastic thing I've seen. Since we're most likely about to die, enjoying each other's company is probably a good thing… in you go.'

'No, not the lid. No. No.'

He tried to keep his arms free and out of the tube, but the man just shoved on the top of his head, until doing that pushed his head so far down into the tube that his arms were dragged in too.

'Useful head you've got there.'

All he could do to stop the lid getting put on him was to hang on to the man's arm so he couldn't get it back out.

'Right little bugger, aren't you. All right, you asked for it. On with the fumes evacuator. Right about now a huge sucker is starting up at the bottom end of your tube. I'd let go of me if I were you, and hang onto your pants… Woops, I think that noise meant it's too late.'

All he cared about was not being shut inside this tube. His pants were still there, tangled around his ankles and sucked down tight, holding his feet to the bottom end of the tube.

'Good idea that,' said the man dragging his arm free, 'Comfy in there, are we?'

He didn't know what else to do, so he started screaming, in fear, in panic, and from hurt feelings that he would be treated like this.

'Flippin' hell! Have you got any idea what you're doing to my ears?... Sorry kid, but I'm hoping this is sound proof.'

On screwed the lid. Around, and around. It was dark inside. The tube was an uncomfortably close fit. He couldn't even turn his arms above his head to wriggle them down past his body, to get his pants back up. The fume evacuator squirted air in underneath him, and then sucked it away again, making all his clothes flop, up, and down. He could hear the man outside.

'All right Ear Buster, thanks for stopping. Let's see if we can't make you more comfortable… Inspection switch. Hey! How's that! Now we can see.'

The walls had gone clear, instead of dull black, and he could see the man outside, hand waiting over a keypad.

'Nup. Think that's about it… Make rubbish cooler if it's likely to go off… I reckon you went off already… Pull your undies up at least brat, I can see your doodle.'

The man was looking back at his flight screen. Motionless, thinking. Suddenly reaching over to tap the tube.

'Hey, you can hear me? If you need to be sick, or nervous wee or something, aim it down the tube, okay?... Good. Rough flying time. I'm sorry Buster. You can howl if you have to.'

The man was looking at him. Not moving, just looking. Obviously thinking again. Maybe if you were out in space by yourself for three years, you did a lot of thinking to yourself. The man was unstrapping himself from his pilot seat now, and looking unhappy.

'Not good enough Viv – he's only a little tacker, like a raw egg. Two elliptoids and a snap flick, and you'll just be cleaning up a broken mess. Bloody hell, <u>why</u> now?'

The man was undoing a lid in the rear bulkhead. Getting out clothes. Lid back on, turning around.

'We're going to try again, you and I,' said the man unscrewing the tube, 'My name's Viv. I'm a scout. Out you come. Can't have you caught with your pants down, hey. This little craft is called a Stingray. They, that ship out there, they would want it whole, so they can find out how to catch all our other scout ships… No, we need to do them up a bit better than that, so they don't end up where they were before. The only way they'll get my ship is if they knock me out first, and then they'd still have to find it. Arms up.'

'Why? It's <u>too</u> big.'

'We are going to pad you out into a big soft ball, so we can rock and roll like mad to get out of here, and you'll stay safe… how's that! Six of my undervests, and you look as snug as a caterpillar in its cocoon. I'll just tie these onto your head with a sock… There.'

'You shouldn't put undies on people's heads, even if they are clean.'

He was starting to really disapprove of the things this man was doing to him.

'No. Quite right. Sorry, but that's the best you and I can do, for now. Not so bad though – your face is just the right size to stick out a leg hole. Up you go, and in. Now we'll just pad your head a bit more. I hope you don't chuck, because this is <u>all</u> my clean under stuff. We'll leave your arms free – just tuck your fingers around into little fists when we're moving, okay?'

'I have to see. I have to <u>see</u>.'

'Keep your hair on… How's that?'

Lid screwing on again.

'Hey in there, if you see me reach for that dull red button, it means things have got hopelessly bad, and we are about to get the hell out of here, so expect screaming weirdness of speed, okay? I don't want that to happen – we'll keeping still and quiet now because I'm hoping that they'll give up and go home… Probably not, since now I'm thinking they trashed your ship deliberately, so they could leave you needing to be rescued, as bait. In fact, I'm sure of it. Not allowing family ships to be armed is pretty dumb. You couldn't even put up a fight to save yourselves. If we get away safely I'm reporting them for this, big time, and then hopefully, next time one of our cruisers catches sight of them, they'll blow the f… okay, that's long enough for waiting around – time to make a dash for safety.'

The pilot was strapping himself back in. Legs, body. A see-through screen folded down in front of him.

'See my screen, kid? Cool hey. Works on brainwaves. It's so I can see everywhere without turning my head. I just think – I wish I could see something… umm… and there's your face. It's real good if you've been out in space for months by yourself, and you're paranoid something's behind you. Okay, my left arm is in, about to click in the right arm, and then we'll see what's happening outside.'

Something smashed against the little scout craft, hard. The pilot's loose arm flew up and hit him in the face. The arm fell down limp next to the seat.

The pilot's head rolled to one shoulder.

And then, nothing.

ATTACKED

The little Stingray was turning slowly around in space. Drifting. The pilot was slumped in his seat, right arm dangling down to the deck. Something was touching along the hull on the outside. Rubbing. Bumping. This wasn't good. The pilot's head screen was blank. The pilot should be thinking red button, red button, to get the little craft away. Soon, like sometimes in Planetman, bad things would happen. He took a big breath, and yelled,

'Wake up, pilot man.'

His voice sounded all right on the wake up bit, but went weak and high after that, because he was worried. Being chicken soft because I'm scared isn't going to stop bad things happening to me, he thought. He tried again, more determined, making his voice low and rough, and so loud that it hurt his throat. Nothing changed out there in the cockpit. He kicked and hit the inside of the tube. The pilot wouldn't wake up. He yelled again. This was worse than when the escape pod wouldn't close – he couldn't even do a brave thing if he wanted to. What to do? What to do? '<u>Daddy</u>, I don't know what to <u>do</u>? <u>MUMMY</u>?' He screamed, crying, and then suddenly he was back in control.

He had to get out of this tube. He pushed and pushed. There were ribs on the back of the lid. The edges of them were hurting his hands, stopping him pushing as hard as he could. He thought about that, and then he began shoving sideways against them, turning, turning. His arms were the right size for this.

Something moved the Stingray, making it tilt, like it was being lined up to go in something. Then he saw a heatball begin in the air, in the middle of the cockpit. He always thought they were a made up thing by the cartoon people, but he could see a shimmering, then a fuzziness, and then the tiny opaque orange spot in mid-air that was the start of it. Hissing, shimmering the air in the cockpit, and suddenly, warmness. He could feel the change even from inside his tube. It wasn't Planetman outside. You couldn't just open a hatch and say 'I give up'. Space was out there, and a big ship that didn't care if he was alive or dead. A big ship from somewhere strange that was trying to kill the pilot. He would die long before the pilot, because he was small. He had come close to death already today, but he still didn't know much about dying, except that it was supposed to be painful, and make you horribly sad. He didn't want to feel any more sad than he was already. He had to get this lid off. He strained, grunting with effort. A noisy fart squeaked out of him. It didn't matter – there was no-one to know. On the next turn the lid slid around easier than he expected, and fell off. He wriggled madly like an over-excited worm, getting himself free from the tube. He fell out on his padded head. His body was still tangled up in six of the man's under vests. The cockpit was hot. The heatball was crackling, and making everything glow orange. Soon it would be burning the pilot man's face. He lifted the pilot's loose arm, and clipped it into its holder.

'Wake up Pilot Man,' he said in his best caring voice, close to the man's ear.

The pilot still wouldn't wake up. There were more noises on the hull of the Stingray, like big chains were being dragged across it, and wrapped around. Or were they clamping things on, to force the outside hatch open? The cockpit lining above the heatball began to buckle, and bubble. A screech screech screech alarm started, tearing at his ears. Smoke, or steam, was coming off things, stinging his eyes. With each moment, everything was getting worse, and even worse.

'Please. Please wake up,' he begged, shaking the pilot.

A dribble of blood ran out the pilot man's nose, but he wouldn't wake up.

Some-one should press that red button. He would have to do it. All by himself. Right now. Shuffling, hurrying around behind the pilot's seat. Tripping over, legs tangled in the vests. Trying to stand up, tripping over, trying to stand, falling flat on his face again. Smoke was coming from above his eyes. From his head. The outer layer of padding the pilot had put on him was trying to catch fire. There was no time left for more standing up attempts.

He started baby crawling forwards frantically, in a tumbling rolling tangled mess. Now he was close enough to reach out and up, towards the controls console. It was hot up there.

'Ouw.'

He pulled his hand back… No, he had to do this. He knew he had to do this, but it was going to hurt. He reached out again.

Changed his mind. It was too hot up there. He heard a frizzing noise, and smelt burnt hair – the pilot man's eyebrows, frizzling into nothing. He stood up as fast as he could, looking around for that button. Where is it, where is it? Pressed. Pressed.

I did it, I did it. Ducking back down, curling himself up into the vests for protection from the heat. Now? Wasn't something supposed to happen? Just the nasty smell of burnt hair, and he could hear sizzling that sounded like melting, bubbling flesh.

WILD ESCAPE

He had pressed the emergency button? He huddled himself on the floor, not understanding why nothing had happened, then he jumped, as three huge explosions rocked the little scout ship, followed by non stop shattering bangs, as it surged forward faster and faster, and then a roaring noise began behind him. He didn't need strapping in – he was squashed up hard against the rear bulkhead so tight his eyes felt like they were being flattened into his head. His ears whistled, singing a crazy out of tune tune. Dizzy. Faint feeling. He realised he was going to start sleeping, even though he didn't want to, because he couldn't breathe. The accelerating speed changed, and he slid down the bulkhead onto the deck. Dark spots were dancing in front of his eyes. Some sort of ray weapon was sweeping over the little scout craft, making all the controls inside shimmer. He didn't feel like he was getting burnt, just sort of shivery tingly all over, like he needed a wee. The roaring of the stingray's escape engines turned into a non-stop scream, and then the Stingray began to wobble, suddenly darting in odd directions, like in a game of chasey. The stars outside the forward screen were racing all over the blackness like a team of crazy white fireworks. Inside the cockpit the shimmering from the ray danced all over everything too. Nothing was staying still long enough for the ray weapon to lock on. He felt like he was in a game. He was the ball thing that bounces around. He wished he'd screwed that lid from the loose rubbish tube back on – it was dangerous. He grabbed it the third time it hit him, and jammed it in under one of the pilot's seat straps on the way past. He would have been safer if he was back in that tube, but he couldn't get himself there because he was flying around out of control, bashing into everything. It was a clever little ship. He could hear it doing all sorts of tricks – firing volleys of things out the back, hissing gasses, and working servo motors to adjust things, maybe armour plates, or reflectors. It knew something was loose inside, and it was steering around in space to keep him in the middle of the back bulkhead, just above the slide tube hatch. It accelerated even more when he was there. He did his best to stay there. Things steadied down, and after ages of nothing but the high-speed screaming roar, he fell asleep.

NOT SAFE TO LAND

A change of direction woke him. There was a murky green dot ahead on the forward screen. It was getting bigger. Thin dark lines of dried blood were all over the pilot man's face, spreading out from his nose. Along the edge of the soft helmet his hair was frizzed up funny, and the pilot's eyebrows weren't there any more, much. He reached out. They felt bristly, like a toothbrush. The face didn't look burnt though, just asleep. If that green thing on the forward screen kept getting closer, the pilot would have to wake up to steer them around it. He reached up and put a hand on the pilot's forehead, gently stroking with his hand, like mother did, when he or his sisters were sick. The pilot wasn't going to wake up, but it might help him get better, for waking up later.

The green thing looked huge now. It was a planet. Blotchy motley gassy looking. They were going to miss it. No, they were turning in, harder and harder. As the little ship swerved left, he was squeezed tight against the right bulkhead with so much pressure he couldn't even lift his fingers away from the cockpit wall. He could feel his face going out of shape, and spit dribbling out of his forced open lips. The Stingray was slowing hard, and dropping down so fast he felt <u>really</u> off. Now was the time he couldn't keep his breakfast in. It was being squashed out of him from both ends.

'Someone <u>change</u> its friggin <u>nappy</u>!' the pilot yelled, before he realised where he was.

Spit was dribbling from the pilot's mouth too. He was thinking again. The head screen was showing the empty tube. The slide hatch. And now him, the boy, squashed here against the cockpit side.

'You okay Buster?'

'Yes,' he wheezed. It was hard to speak, because his lungs were too squashed by sideways pressure to get air.

'I'll just find out where we're landing… No. Not here…not allowed, and it's a poisonous dump. Okay, we're going to pancake the atmosphere to knock off any tailroids… Hang on tight.'

Drifts of dirty green cloud were flashing past. The stingray was doing sharp bounces, down, up, and to each side. They were sinking into the cloud, deeper and deeper. Now everything in the forward screen was murky green, and getting dark. How did the pilot know where to go? He felt suddenly scared, a chilling nervousness going through him: some patches of green ahead were darker than others. What if the stingray was about to hit something? Please, don't go any deeper. His head spun around in fear. Something was coming in close. He could see it on the sidescreen, moving with them in the murkiness. Something that had the spikes of weapons in the shape of its shadow. He tapped the pilot's arm. The pilot looked, put a finger over his lips in the shush sign, then whispered.

'Going up now.'

The Stingray was good at doing things quickly, and in big amounts. He was being squished into the deck of the cockpit this time. He felt like he weighed so much that every part of him was too heavy to move. A bubble gurgled around in his stomach, and then a super huge burp came out of him. The pilot chuckled, and said 'Shhh'. They were rising up through the green faster and faster. The stingray's engine was making a roaring that rose to a long scream, there was a pow noise, and, sudden silence. They were out in space again. The stingray had stopped being so rough to be inside.

'Well done little man! You are the best co-pilot I ever had. Smooth flying from now on. Just having a check of things… Okay, let's get ourselves cleaned up.'

The pilot was flicking his seat straps off.

'Through the slide tube, and then we'll start with your britches: they're a bit powerful for a small space like this… Hmmm, and my face. Ugly frightening, but it's only a blood nose that got to run in all directions.'

They went through the tube into the main cabin. The pilot unclipped a small container from a bulkhead and sprayed his face.

'That's better. Took the sting out of it. Okay, britches off. Err! Pooey!'

'_You_ shut up.'

'You know they've got surveillance systems on that planet that can pick up what flies say to each other while they're making out. Wonder what they made of your burp.'

His clothes were put inside a shallow thing with a long thin lid, like his mother's. You laid the clothes out flat like they were a lying down person, squashed the lid shut on them, and waited – neutralizing oils, rinsing out, drying. Three things, each one making a left to right squirting, hissing noise, inside the machine.

'All right, let's see… open the lid, and everything should be clean and dry. Not bad, hey. Quick wipe of you… You get dressed while I check the incoming messages. You can do that by yourself?'

'I'm not _that_ small.'

It was okay to say, but he was having trouble with the ship runners, and had to go back through the slide tube to ask.

'The tightening bits won't scrunch up right.'

'No problem. There you go. Look at this: they analysed your burp. They reckon I've got prohibited wildlife on board – a Jehovian dink squirrel.'

'What does one of them look like?'

'No idea. Let's see if it's in the ship's data… Oh. Don't worry about it – it was just their joke.'

'<u>How</u> was it a joke?'

'All right cranky pants, let's see… "a derogatory name for a small child, originating in the Deep History of Blue Skies One. Generally used on pesky, cheeky, nuisance children, as a backhanded term of endearment". See, not so bad – it means they liked you.'

'<u>Where</u> does it say that? I'm not stupid. I can read: "…to des-scribe product of ill conceived, genetically mis-matched alliance, formed because of wild sex-u-al grat… grat…<u>tification</u>".'

'Hey, come on, no need to get upset. That was really good reading for someone as small as you. It's not as complicated as it sounds anyway. It just means that people had so much fun making the baby that the kid is probably going to be a bit wild too. That's not a bad thing, is it? Well, Jehovian dink squirrel, let's see what you think of Scout food. Ship's biscuits, and dryblock water.'

The biscuit was like eating a crumbly piece of a building. The water looked like a lump of stone too. It went in a thing that squashed it with heaps of pressure, and suddenly the bottle filled with water, and the small stone was gone.

He nibbled the biscuit, and sucked at the edge of his drink tumbler. The man was watching him.

'What do you think?'

'I want my Mum and Dad.'

'I know you do. I meant: what do you think of the biscuit.'

'<u>No,</u>' he said firmly in reply, meaning this biscuit wasn't allowed to be food.

He was sitting on the deck, back leaning against one side of the cockpit, nibbling the tasteless biscuit and looking around at everything. The pilot was sitting on the other side, looking at him. In the middle was the pilot's seat, empty.

'My turn?' he asked.

'What?' asked the pilot, surprised and nearly laughing.

'My turn to have a go of driving us,' he explained.

'You are like four or something! You can't even... you just can't, all right.'

'I'm <u>five</u>, and I can do lots of things.'

'Okay okay. Gees, sor-ry.'

The pilot pulled the display screen down and around, and began watching something. It didn't make sense looking at it from the back.

'You are a champion red button presser,' the pilot said after a while.

'Can I look?'

'Okay. Over here then. Wait, wait: I'm just telling it to go back a bit, and... hey! You don't have to sit <u>on</u> me. Better.'

The screen looked like a crowded jumble of lots of things. He looked up at the pilot, hoping he would fix it. The pilot began explaining it instead.

'It's a record of what happens in the ship, all the readouts and settings on the controls, and above them is like a fisheye lens picture of what happens in the cockpit. There you are, crawling around, your head smoking, and... pressing the escape button. That was pretty ace for a four year old.'

He knew the pilot was stirring him, for fun, so he ignored the 'for a four year old' remark.

'I can do stuff,' he said, touching the control stick in front of the pilot seat with his outstretched fingers.

He wanted to steer it around like a playvision game.

'Yep. You sure can. Thanks kid. I reckon we are like evens: I saved you, and then you saved us.'

He stood up for a look around. There was a dot ahead in the forward screen. Yellow this time. Dry summer grass yellow. Getting larger like the green one did. The chance to have a go of piloting the little ship was gone. He decided to get in that tube before things got bad rough in the cockpit again.

'No, kid – you'll be right. Up on the pilot seat with me and we'll fly us in. I'll take her down gently this time.'

The pilot strapped his legs and body in again.

'Up you come.'

'Arms,' he ordered the pilot.

The pilot hadn't strapped his arms in, again.

'No thanks Bossyboots. Arm locks are only for wild stuff, and then I steer using these buttons on the seat under my hands. It's hard work and no fun.'

The controls were too big, and too far away. He could only just reach them.

'Shutting down the autopilot now. I forgot how small kids are. How about out on the end of my knees. How's that? You stay between my arms and hold the controls below my hands, and we'll do this together… Yeah. Not bad, hey?'

'I would do it better if it was just me?' he said hopeful, and joking, stirring the pilot back.

'So you reckon,' said the pilot, 'This planet's called Outer 17. Not much this, not much that. Bit dry. Bit boring. We won't be here long – me to send the report through, tidy the cockpit lining, and re-pack the back end, and you for your family to come. You've probably got lots of Aunts and Uncles out there looking for you already… Here we go.'

RESCUE JOURNEY OVER, BUT WHAT COMES NEXT?

A big tube tower was sticking up from the surface of the planet. They were flying down towards it in smaller and smaller circles, sinking through the sky, and now dropping into its wide round mouth, and then down, and around, and around, and down, and down. The big hole at the top shrank until it looked like a small circle of daylight high above them. Slowing. Turning. The pilot was parking the Stingray on a metal balcony. He flicked switches, and the boy heard the outer hatch hiss open.

'Through the slide tube we go,' said the pilot.

They stood outside for a while in front of a metal door, but it didn't open.

'Deck heating's been put on at least,' said the pilot, crouching down to touch the floor, 'so someone knows we're here'.

They sat on the edge of the balcony, legs out under the safety rail, and waited.

'Do you know Planetman?' he asked finally, 'I know he's only a cartoon,' he added like an apology.

'Sure do. Planetman is what got me wanting to be a scout. I had this Planetman doll robot thing, when I was a bit older than you, it could fly, not much, but a bit. I loved that thing like a true, real-life friend. Better even.'

'Mine just had bendy arms and legs.'

'Not bad.'

They watched the afternoon grow old while they discussed toys they'd had, and playvision games they liked.

The air was getting cooler, and the daylight at the top of the tube tower going dim. There was a noise. They both looked around. The door onto the balcony was finally opening.

'I'm sorry I'm sorry,' a lady was saying in a hurry as she came out of the door, 'We don't get many off planet visitors, well, none really, except during Crew Parade week, and then it's all at once. We've all worked here for years, but not one of us knew the code for the Scout Ship Landing... Welcome to Outer 17.'

HEAVY GOODBYE

'I can't take you on with me little man. There's no room, and it isn't safe. I'd just be going further and further away from where your family could find you.'

So this was it? He was getting dumped in this strange place.

'You did a good thing for me up there, Tuff Stuff. Thanks, okay? Well, I guess this is it. Bye Kid. Thanks for being fun.'

A pat on the head and the scout ship pilot began walking away, then he hesitated, and turned around. The daylight glinted on the gold of the ancient lady ring on his hand as he walked back. It was one of those strange details you remember all your life, for no reason. Something is triggered in your mind, and your memories make a special place.

'Give us a hug, little fella... Where-ever I am out there I will always remember you.'

The pilot walked to the lift. Went in. Pressed buttons on the lift wall. The doors closed. The lift was going to take the pilot way way up the tube, then he would go back out on that balcony, climb into his little craft, and fly away. Another person gone. First it was Mum and Dad, then his sisters, then Planetman, and now the pilot. He was so lonely he was scared.

UNWANTED ON A STRANGE PLANET, WITH NO WAY HOME

A woman was talking behind him.

'No… no. No. We are not a dumping ground for space orphans… Find some charity that does then… No, I don't know how many in the last ten years… So what if it's one. He's a nice quiet little boy called Mark. It can't be that hard for you to find him a home. Where do <u>our</u> unwanted kids go? Yes, good idea, you phone around. He'll be waiting out the front.'

MRS BENSON AND THE CHILDREN'S HOME

'Well, my little space orphan, what do you think?'

'I want my Mum.'

'Yes… My name is Mrs Benson, and because the universe is such a big place to find a little boy in, you'll be staying with me for a while.'

'How big is this while?'

'Oh…about as long as it takes. How about I tell you a story about another little space orphan, just like you. His name was Alito Magnificus. He had straight hair, and sturdy little fingers, just like those.'

'I don't want a story. I want my Mum.'

'One day, his parents took him down to the royal armoury, and said, "Times are looking bad for our planets, armourer. We must concentrate on things we really care about. You must stop building impregnable fortresses and unbreakable weapons, because we are worried that in the storms of war we will lose Alito. We want you to make <u>him</u> impregnable, and unbreakable, so when we find him again, he will still be in one piece." "I will", said the armourer proudly. He was much better with living things than with white concrete, and dark metals. He looked at all Alito's atoms, every single one, where they were in his body. Then he looked at the rest of the universe, and where everything else was, and he thought hard. "Alito! I have the answer", he said, very happy. He was even a little proud. When he finished Alito, he thought he might do the Emperor, and the Lady Emperor, and then his own wife, and their little girl, and the nice lady down the street, and himself of course, and then everyone would be safe from war. "Alito <u>first</u>", said Alito's mum and dad, because the armourer sometimes got so excited he didn't finish things properly. Alito didn't feel any different the day he was finished, but his atoms inside him were dancing around by themselves now, separate from everything else in the universe. "Alito, I am very proud of you", said the armourer, "but before we go and show everybody, I have to tell you something. See this bottle? If you are ever lost for a long time, you must drink some of this. Then you won't get any hungrier, or thirstier, while you wait. I have another bottle in the armoury to make you a hungry, thirsty boy again". He put the bottle belt around Alito's middle, and did it up, and then they set out for the Royal halls. They hadn't got very far when they met a military man. He was a kind old man who flew around the universe stopping wars. He said, "Alito must come with me. This world is no longer the right shape for children to be…'

'Why is he called Alito. <u>That's</u> not a proper name.'

'It is, for little princes. Princes have special names, like Alito, and Fabrillus, and Mark…'

'Ha! That is <u>not</u> a prince's name. Princes don't get called that.'

'They do, if they are very brave little boys… So the old man walked with Alito out of the palace, out of the city, and away into a field, among the trees and flowers. There was a strange light in the sky, and when they looked back there was no city, and no palace, not at all, not any more for in all of Time. The old man said to Alito, "Life is very big. If you fall out of your happiness, you must find another happiness to climb into." "But my family are all gone", wailed Alito. He was a very unhappy little prince. "Families are never gone, not all of us", said the old man, "We are hidden in all sorts of odd places.

Family are people who make room for you in their lives. Would you like to be family with me for a while, until you find some new happiness to climb into?" Alito didn't answer, because he was thirsty and hungry. He drank from his special bottle and felt much better… So little fellow, how about you drink up your cocoa, and feel a little better, hmm?'

'Being brave is a <u>bad</u> thing.'

'Yes. You don't have to be brave any more. What would you like to be?'

'I'm going to be on a <u>big</u> ship, and <u>fly</u>… <u>everywhere</u>, and I'm going to find <u>my</u> family. <u>My</u> Mum, and <u>my</u> Dad, and <u>my</u> sisters.'

'Yes Mark, little man, I do hope so.'

He cried for days and days, quietly to himself. He stood at an upstairs window of the Children's Home looking far away to the horizon, making hurt little animal noises. Outside was flat, dirt, rubbly nothing. The buildings around the Children's Home had been wrecked to the ground, or carted away. In the distance was the breeze tube up on its stilts, and beyond that, the rooftops of houses. Not manufactured modern houses, but build where they were from bits ones. He could tell by the shapes of the rooves. Even further away, he could see dimly in the heat haze the shapes of large buildings. He kept his father's ship's watch with him, every minute of every day. He was terrified he would lose it, forever, and he would have nothing left of home. Mrs Benson said 'You don't need that in the shower', but then he screamed and screamed, and Mrs Benson gave it back.

He was surprised there were no lessons to do each day. Learning things was how he could get himself ready to get off this world and back to his family. He asked. No. Lessons happened at a school, but not for him. There was no money for school clothes, or for fares to go to and from. Food for all the children at the Home came first. He knew everything ahead of him in his life depended on him learning things. He begged her. He said he'd try very hard? What good would that do, Mrs Benson asked, if it meant there wasn't enough food for them all? Then he looked up at her, terror in his eyes that her no was unchangeable.

MRS BENSON SAYS GOODBYE

Mrs Benson gave his hair a ruffle, and he got on the end of the queue. He would have been a happy child. Sometimes, from the silence of his private thoughts, cheeky naughtiness would suddenly burst out of him, surprising everyone. Not enough of those days. She watched him get blown into the people in front of him. He'd never been in a breeze tube before. Stand up little man. That's it. Back on your mat. And away he went. He was a sturdy little fellow. She thought of his first happy words: "Mrs Benson, come and see!… It's tall as anything, but if you push, (grunt grunt) it falls over! BANG! Really loud! We don't have things that fall over, not on <u>our</u> ship", and then she had watched horror stab his heart, as he remembered what happened to his family's ship.

He was gone now. He had her letter, and if he got too cold or hungry, he wasn't to worry about the fare – just take his mat to the tube, and come home. To the Children's Home. She'd done her best. It wasn't enough. She knew that, but this was how it always ended. Like so many children before him he was out in the world now, gone from her life.

THE BREEZE TUBE

Once he was standing up it was fun. You could lean in different directions on your mat, and it would steer around and between the grownups. You could make yourself suddenly surge forward past people, or not, by how you caught the breeze.

'Bloody children,' said a man, but he sounded happy, glad someone was having fun.

The spinning things the floor was made of were making a rattly high-pitched whizzy sound. People were talking. He was looking around at everyone and the view outside, when he ran into a lady. She nearly sat on him, and she wasn't pleased. She stared at his clothes and then reached for him, like she was going to keep him to be taken somewhere. A boring looking man grabbed him first.

'He'll stand quietly with me for a while,' the man told the lady.

She wasn't pleased. She brushed at her dress like he had made it dirty.

'Left children should not be allowed in the tube.'

It wasn't up to her. He rolled along next to the man. The tube was going alongside a small hill now. Outside he could see two boys up on a road, throwing stones. They were trying to throw them over the tube, but not doing very well.

'Children should not be allowed,' stated the woman crossly, as stones plink-plonked onto the outside of the tube. The man stopped a laugh in his throat.

'Can you believe she ever was one?' he asked softly.

'A boy is something I most certainly never was,' she said. 'Sorry. I think I need a new life,' she added, and then she nearly smiled.

He looked right into her face, and saw sadness, and boredom, and distant happy memories. The shadow of her almost smile did him good, running through his insides like sunlight. He couldn't help smiling back.

'You are a little demon,' she said with a half laugh, infected unwillingly by the happiness in his face, and then they were all swirling off the main floor, onto a station landing.

SCHOOL

He liked the school. Some things were like he remembered; the coloured writers, and a 'how tall are you now?' poster. Seeing familiar things made him feel a tiny bit closer to his family.

At morning playtime a man was walking towards him, with Mrs Benson's letter in his hand.

'Come here boy. Is this true?'

He didn't know what Mrs Benson had written, so what could he say? He looked up at the man, hoping the next words wouldn't be bad.

'I need to know, from you, that you want to be here.'

This was like home too. It would start with having fun, things would get a bit wild, then Dad would say those words 'I need to know that you…' Something would get confiscated, or he wouldn't be allowed to do something, for a while. The only thing he had to lose was being here. He looked up again at the man, thinking 'please don't let it be this. Please, please…'.

'All right little man, I'm taking that look as a yes… You'll be in my class, because I can't ask teachers to teach for free. I'm thinking, looking into your little face, that you are a budding "extracted" anyway.'

Mr Arthurs' class was mostly boys, boys that had made the other teachers angry one too many times by mucking around and being cheeky. They were the 'extracted' children, the ones taken out of normal classes so they could be watched extra, to help them behave themselves. Mr Arthurs was the boss of the school, and did school boss things at a desk while they did their work. There were five boys the same size. They were whispering, and giggling. Without looking up Mr Arthurs was talking.

'Why are we here?'

'Because being a boy can be very annoying for other people,' chanted the five of them.

'Precisely. On with your work.'

HOME IS WHEREVER YOU HIDE YOURSELF

When everyone left for the day he stayed, and slept in the space between the shelter-shed and the back fence, on his breeze tube mat. It was his home away from the Home. He spent the late afternoons trying to imagine how someone his age could get back into space. And when those thoughts ran out he thought of things it might be good to collect to help him travel the Universe. The one time he held a coin in his hand was because he found it in the sandy dirt of the playground. It was a glorious feeling. He was like everyone else – he had money to spend. In the happiness of the moment he forgot about collecting it for travelling the Universe. He was walking around the school building to go and see what this coin could buy him at the tuck shop, when he heard James crying. Not sook crying, unhappiness. He didn't know what to say, or do, so he just stood there, waiting.

'I lost it. I can't go now,' said James, and then he started crying again, hurting a lot inside.

The coin was warm and round in his hand. He said goodbye to it with his heart, and lifted his arm. James looked, then reached slowly out, took the coin, and held it to his chest while he sat there, thinking his own thoughts.

For a moment in time they were kindred spirits; they both knew the world could be a private lonely unhappy place, and that the other boy understood. That was all. The magic of the coin was gone, back to where it belonged. His collection of things to help him travel the Universe had shrunk back to the breeze mat, and the ship's watch.

The Children's Home was so far that he would begin walking after school on Friday, and not get there until all the other kids at the Home were asleep, and the wall clock said it was nearly Saturday. He liked the journey because it was long, and nearly all he could manage. And he liked how surprised and happy Mrs Benson was to see him. He always set out skipping, hopping, running from side to side of the path, but after a while, usually not long after dark, it turned into a slog. His legs would complain, but he'd just stride out with longer steps, and they'd settle back into it, then some muscle bits would ache, but he'd keep on walking. He would look up at the breeze tube overhead, and wonder at how simple it was. Just a big clear tube, wide enough for lots of people, with a floor in it of little balls on rods that could spin how they liked. The people blew along inside. He watched them to distract himself from the effort of the walk, until the rough path underneath his feet headed off into the darkness, away towards the Children's Home. Walking walking, walking. Finally his knees would go watery weak, like they had nothing left. They wouldn't do what that they were told – went wobbly if he asked too much. After that happened he would walk with them slowly and gently, glad of each step. If he kept on walking he got there in the end. It seemed to echo what his heart knew – that his life was a long journey, and inside that journey was another adventure, up there in the dark, between all those stars. If he didn't give up, if he just kept on going, then one day he would be up there again with his family.

LEARNING, AND YEARNING

During the week in the evenings he climbed the shelter-shed and sat on the roof. He looked up at the stars and wondered where Mum and Dad were. He watched lights come on in the houses. All the families were happy and warm together. Then one by one the lights went out. It would get cold, and he would climb back down into the space between the shed and the fence, to sleep.

Food each day was school lunch. Every morning, all morning, his stomach would be gnawing at him, telling him he needed to eat, making him feel thin and cold. Then, finally, at lunchtime, it felt so good to be full of food that he would go a bit silly, and that would get him detention, when he was supposed to be getting after school help with his work.

'I know you're a special case boy, but this is a two way effort, and if that's the best you can do, you'd better find yourself a job now as a boy apprentice, because there'll be no assistance grant. Big school and High college still to go, and you think you'll get there by acting the goat. We're all trying our hardest for you, but the way you're going, you'll grow up into a lonely young man, without a place in the world – no family, no future.'

'I don't care.'

But he cared more than anything. He had nightmares that Mum and Dad were floating away through empty darkness, cold and dead. He knew his sisters were out there. They were probably by themselves, like him. He couldn't bear the thought of them waiting for him to come, and then nothing. He knew what that felt like – waiting, hoping that some-one who cared about you wouldn't forget you.

'Mr Arthurs, I do care? Please?'

'All right lad. I was packing up for the day, not giving up. Did you take that note home? Hmm, well, it's winter, and school jumpers aren't optional.'

He had a book he'd found on the shelf in Mr Arthurs' room – 'Construction of Repeat Use Interplanetary Projectiles'. He was allowed to read it, but not during class. The pictures weren't too hard. There was a really good one of a little craft the shape of a writing pen, meant for sending only one person. He had no way of starting to make any of the parts for it. It was hard enough just drawing his own version of the picture. When he found that book he had felt excited, like now he could finally get started on some good plans for his future. He closed it sadly. He could dream about it, but it wasn't going to get him home. Lessons were happening around him. He began watching and listening.

World history. This world was generally flat, mostly dry, and boring. The rest of space had no reason to be interested in it, and only the kids seemed to care that the whole of space was out there. He looked around the class. Not one of them had been off this planet, none of these kids, not one teacher, and probably no-one's parents, either.

'Not all worlds are the same. We heard last week how Lefty's planet only allows two children per family, and when his mother gave birth to twins, well, with Lefty, how many children in their family did that make? Yes Bernard, that made three, so his parents had to make a very difficult decision – wait around for the government to come and take one of his baby sisters' lives away, or risk the whole family, by becoming space refugees. Our world too has characteristics peculiar to it, in climate, landscape, and social structuring. What are the main features of Outer 17?... Yes Dennis.'

'We are the only right size planet for living on, in this part of space?'

'And?'

'We don't have anything special for people to fight over?'

'Mr Arthurs, Mr Arthurs…we've got the Academy!'

'Yes, thank you James. So – Outer 17, supports complex Life, has no valuable resources, and has the Lifeworlds Space Academy. Three good reasons why we are a safe and secure planet. All right. That's enough for today. Those of you who didn't have erasers, get them by tomorrow.'

SOMETHING BETTER THAN SCHOOL

Erasers, by tomorrow. No hope of that happening. Almost every day some new thing came up that he was supposed to go back to the Children's Home and ask Mrs Benson for. He couldn't.

Asking only made her unhappy. This was hard too. Why didn't they go home? They were standing over there in a group. He'd accepted that they didn't want to be friends. He knew their names, their loyalties to each other, and, after a while, could see the real boy inside each of them, behind the acting up, and the noise. James daydreamed, about everything. Shane watched, expecting unfairness to happen, and then he would make a silent decision to make the best of things. Philip… Dennis… Bernard. He sat in the same classroom every day with all of them, but that was all. He had nothing. They had pocket games to show, tuck shop food to share, each other's places to go around to to watch Planetman, and to play. They weren't thin and cold, and wearing strange worn out clothes. He sat down on a big weed against the fence, and thought of other times, other places. Often he thought of his sisters in the escape pod, not even looking at him, because they knew he was looking after them. They were sure he had everything under control. I can be that, he thought, but this was very hard right now. One of the boys was coming over. Shane. Standing close. Looking down.

'I have to give you this. My mum said.'

An old school jumper.

'I'm sorry. It wasn't my idea. My mum made me.'

They were watching. Something more was going on.

'Thanks,' he said softly, and hugged it to him.

'So it's okay to give you stuff?… I've got better stuff than old jumpers you can have… James wants to know if you like sleeping behind the shelter-shed, or if you just have to.'

They were all coming closer. Standing over him.

'We know you do. We used to get changed there, until it turned into like, your bedroom!'

'Lefty, why do you come to school, if you haven't got money for anything?' asked Bernard.

Mark answered looking at his own feet, talking softly to his worn out shoes.

'Because I'm going out in space to find my family. You have to go to school to do that.'

That was the cold truth. Out of everything, he knew that for certain. If he didn't get through school he'd be trapped on this planet his whole life, and his sisters, and his mum and dad, would get old and die where-ever they were, thinking, the whole time, that he didn't even try. That he didn't care. The boys were staring down at him like he was a mouse they'd cornered.

'You have to go to better than school.'

'We go to something better than school.'

'Shut up Shane. You're just making it worse for him.'

They were walking away, arguing.

'Well you are. He can't come. You have to have money, and a uniform. Where's he getting that from, hey?'

'Miss Shandy said everyone's allowed. I asked.'

'Oh yeah. Good one James. See you suckers there.'

They were splitting up.

They'd turned the corner of the school buildings, but he could still hear their voices. Where were they going?

Three of them stopped in a back lane. Dumped their school backpacks down on the road. Started taking off clothes. No wonder they were always warmer than him: white underneath stuff that looked soft. There was no white, not for clothes, not at the Home. If it started out white, it ended up rinse-washed light tan, or grey, or the colour of whatever else was in the wash. They were getting other clothes out of their packs. Blue long pants, long sleeve shirts, and caps. They had uniforms.

'I'm going to get my old pants back, for Lefty.'

'Didn't Winston wear them, after he pissed himself?'

'They get washed. Lefty won't care. I was rapt when I got my uniform, and it was like only Alan's old crap.'

'Yeah, sucked in.'

'Mum put my shirt in. I can get that out. It was mine anyway… but the emergency clothes bin never has runners?'

'Yeah well, like Miss Shandy says, fight one battle.'

They were all sitting down on the dusty lane, and pulling ship runners onto their feet. People on planets didn't wear ship runners.

'Yeah. But Lefty's not allowed to sook all the time.'

'He doesn't! Sometimes he's like wicked fun.'

'Like when?'

'Like when Miz Anderson gave us that talk about "The Disadvantaged People", and she's waddling out of the room, doing her "I'm the most important person, and I'm leaving" act.'

'And Lefty cracked it!'

'This runner's got dog poo on it... well, what happened?'

'Were you having a sicky? I thought everyone was there.'

'He snuck up behind her, and full arm swing smacked her on the bum... It wasn't funny. It was real scary. She went white faced. They were looking at each other, both upset to the max.'

'And then she says, "are you sorry", and he goes, "if you are", and she says yes, and lifts him up for this great big hug. She like won't touch us, because she thinks boys are germs.'

'And then, for the whole rest of the day, he's like crazy happy, and so funny. Nobody mucks around like him. He goes like volume eleven.'

'On the last warnings list, he...'

'Yeah! While Mr Arthurs was talking to that teacher at the door,'

'...he snuck up and wrote "Mr Arthurs", for "being not enough fun".'

'And Arthurs goes, "Oh yes, and what would be more fun?".'

'Outside,' Lefty goes, like "let's do it now".'

'And Mr Arthurs goes "Hmmm. So it was you Lefty. All right, ten minutes more maths, and then outside for a game of batball".'

'I wish he was like that every day,' said James, as they were all standing back up, ship runners on their feet.

'Who? Lefty or old Arthurs,' asked Bernard.

'Both of them,' answered Shane.

Lefty – a child left at a Home, because no-one wanted it. Mark sat down in the dark against the fence. Lefty. It wasn't his name. He would like to belong to something. He wanted one of those uniforms. He felt a tiny rush of guilt, for Mrs Benson. Without her he would have nothing at all. These clothes he had on were sort of a uniform. They said to the world that he belonged to the Children's Home. He couldn't feel proud of that. He knew what that meant, from the day he went to join the Library. That was a long walk too. He was really excited. The Lady said children were free. When he joined, he was going to use his card on the computer, and go through every rescue in the Space Accidents database until he found his family's ship. Then he could find out what happened. He was standing at the counter looking at all the boxes he was supposed to write in, feeling really pleased he'd thought of this. This was a good day. He was being extra careful to write properly on the joining form, because they turned that part of it into the card that let you use the computer. A man came over, said, 'Thought so,' and took the pen out of his hand. Then the man took the piece of paper away. 'Children's Home', he said to the lady, as he crumpled the membership form in his fist, and threw it into a bin. She was being nice. She held out a jar full of lollies, but she said, 'You can't pay the fines, and books aren't always looked after'. She didn't give the pen back, or a new piece of paper. 'You can use the books when you're here.' 'Computer?' he asked. She didn't answer, but that meant no. He didn't know what to do with the lolly. He couldn't eat it. He felt like it would choke him. He watched it in his hands. Its bright colours were like a little recipe for happiness, but the happiness was for some-one else. He reached up and put it back in the jar. He had to get out of the library because water was starting to spill from his eyes. That was a horrible day. He had learnt his old shorts and thin shirt were a uniform that told the world how to treat him. He remembered being rock-hard determined to go back and ask again when that man wasn't there, but the librarian lady caught up with him outside. 'No need to cry. I can look something up for you?' She could tell it was important. He explained. 'Oh Sweetheart,' she said when he'd finished, like she wanted to cry now, 'that database isn't real. It just has big disasters to amaze the children. Space is too big to list everything'.

He looked out into the darkness. While he was remembering things, James Bernard and Shane had gone. He could hear, coming from a block away, the sound of kids having fun. He stood up and began walking. He wouldn't be allowed to join in, but he could watch.

CADET CLUB

It was like the school hall, but it wasn't at school. Kids were mucking around everywhere outside. They were happy. He could smell food. They went inside. The door shut. The windows were too high above the ground. There was nowhere to climb. He was hanging onto a windowsill, doing a chin-up to see in, when, just before his fingers lost their grip, James looked up and saw him. He nearly ran away, but then he thought – so what if I'm here? Nobody said I couldn't be. How come he wasn't even allowed to look at people inside somewhere warm, with food, and other people to do things with – how come he wasn't even allowed to look at happiness? Some-one was opening the door. James.

      'Lefty…quick.'

James was standing halfway out the narrowly opened door, waving bits of uniform.

      'We nicked these back. Give me yours.'

He was inside. James was shutting the door. The lights were bright. The hall was warm. He felt excited. He was going to <u>be</u> something, with everyone else. James was stuffing the Home clothes into his pack on a wall hook.

      'Just say we invited you. It's true anyway, Shane and I wanted to.'

A big fat woman with a large voice made them all sit on the floor, cross-legged.

      'Arms up, not yelling. Any new recruits this week?'

      'Me!' Mark said louder than he meant, and then, as an after thought, shoved his hand in the air.

      'And who brought our new recruit?'

      'They did', he said, pointing.

      'Methinks you need a little training, recruit. All right. Time for our vow… one, two,'

'Cadets are daggy, cadets aren't cool, but cadets is better than "after school". We eat, we shout, we muck about, and at the end of the year, we go up in a space ship.'

The vow didn't rhyme very well, but they didn't care. He liked that.

'Covers off… Everyone up the ladder, I mean, on board our ship,' she said to the group.

She had him by the back of his collar. He wasn't going anywhere.

'Navigator, set a course for the Southern Stars, while I have a talk with our new recruit.'

She was steering him over to an office off the side of the hall. Shutting the door.

'So this is what all the fuss was about – "can we bring a friend… but what if they're this, or that". Lefty, aren't you. I know my boys and girls pretty well. Well enough to know those pants are James', the pair that ripped on the ladder. The shirt is Bernard's, because, my little friend, it says Bernard above the pocket… So you can't bring acceptable food, and you can't pay your clubroom fee… We need to come to an arrangement, don't we? Perhaps you can help me tidy up after, and one afternoon of the week you can help me get things ready. We'll see if that works. Welcome aboard cadet, I'm glad to have you in my crew.'

She was opening the door back into the hall.

'We're a bit short of noisy silly boys at the moment.'

It didn't sound like it.

There was a large wooden platform. Bolted to it was a panel from the bottom of a shuttlebus, a spotlight from a docking bay, the nose cone from something small, and a red tail fin from a fighter trainer. He climbed the ladder. On the platform were broken bits of ships, arranged like they belonged together. A rackset of six bunks, seats in rows, navigation consoles, a nearly complete communications station, and a towline thrower they were pretending was a weapon. He stood at the top of the ladder looking at everyone else having fun. He felt awkward. They might resent him trying to join in. It was like being invisible, standing waiting watching them. He put one foot back on the top of the ladder, but he was still hoping someone might look over.

Everything up here looked like good fun. No-one was looking his way. They were all busy. He decided to go back down the ladder and play by himself.

'Welcome aboard recruit,' called out a grade six boy from school.

'First time on a ship?'

'No. I lived on one,' he answered, taking his foot off the top of the ladder.

They were all looking at him.

'Where is it?'

'It broke.'

'Ships don't break, they crash.'

'It broke. Out in space.'

He suddenly knew he didn't want to talk about it. Not ever. Not with these people. They weren't family. They were waiting. Mouths opening to ask questions, then thinking more instead. Looking at each other, then back at him. If they all kept looking at him he knew he was going to cry, because he had no-one, just himself, and right now that hurt.

'Let's see if supper's ready,' said the grade six boy changing the subject. They all cheered and raced for the ladder, happy to let him keep his private feelings to himself. Maybe they were a little bit family after all.

SEEING A WAY TO AN UNCERTAIN FUTURE

'Did you enjoy tonight?... Good. Thought you did. You're a little tricker, aren't you. Poor James – "Miss Shandy, is he allowed to do it like that, Miss Shandy, he's upside down again, Miss Shandy, some-one's tied my pants loop to the ladder". Just remember, a practical joke is only funny when the person it's done to knows it's done in friendship. Remember that, and I think we're in for a lot of fun. That's all the plates. Mugs next. My father started this little club. Pass me that scourer – I don't know how your little mouths get so filthy that they do this to a cup. He said, "Shandy, there's no dreams left on this planet. Nothing to discover. Children need dreams". What are your dreams?'

He hadn't expected her to stop talking, so the question caught him by surprise. What were his dreams?

'I'm going to find my family. I have to become a <u>real</u> space cadet, and…'

Yes, but then, how was he going to find them?

'Hey hey hey, no tears here.'

'I wasn't.'

'Yes, but I know when something's coming,' she said, combing his hair across with her hand, 'so, about your dream: your plan is a good one. One step at a time, and you've come to the right place. Our ship is called the S.S. Pielojunk, but already it's got two of our cadets into college. Keep moving that teatowel, or we'll be here all night.'

'Do you really know useful stuff?'

'I do. In my day job I clean at the Academy. It's not a very exciting way to earn a living, but while I'm doing it I watch how they train the students, and I see the equipment they train them on. And I have a few ingredients of my own that life taught me, to throw into my girls and boys. Ah well, so that's your dream. I think you should become a navigator, so that you're not relying on other people to help you find your way. What do you think?'

'How do you do that?'

'Little school, big school, High college, and then the Academy. One step at a time. Now, there was something else. What was it Shandy? Oh yes – while I was having a little chat with your Mrs Benson, I thought of this: the Academy have a search computer where you log in what you're after. Then, if anyone can help, they log an entry back. If you would like me to, I will log in you, and your family. Often nothing happens, but if some-one is looking for anything with you or your family's names in it, they will see your entry. Space is a big place, so don't get over-excited. I just thought perhaps it could be a good start.'

'Planetti,' he said eagerly, his family name was Planetti. She was looking at him, like she was having a big thought. There was something wrong with being called Planetti.

'Oh well, never mind. It was a good idea anyway,' she said, as she pulled the plug up and emptied the sink.

He was lost in the moment, looking up at her, waiting to understand.

'Planetti's not a family name, ' she explained.

'Yes it is?' he said, unhappy, uncertain, almost scared, 'Dad said we are all in the Planetti family.'

He didn't have much left, only his dad's ship's watch, and his memories, and he didn't want to let go of any of them.

'Okay then. I will look,' she said, 'but there are many Planetti, all escaping from worlds that aren't for them, and I am sure they are all trying to get back in contact with people they care about, so you and I mustn't get our hopes up. Now if you'd been called Mark McSnarkleberry, spelt with a zee, and perhaps several x's as well for good measure, then I think our search would have been easier.'

'Are there lots of Planetti families?'

'Yes Sweetheart.'

'Too many to find me?'

'We'll see. We don't know that yet.'

THE COLD CAME AND HE WANTED TO DIE

Now it was further into the year the nights were cold. Sometimes really cold. Specially if there were no clouds, like tonight. Miss Shandy had taught him that the most accurate, finely tuned system on any off-planet vessel was the life support. Hard to believe, in a heated hall with the lights on when you were full of hot chocolate and biscuits, but he understood now. He could feel each tiniest degree of more coldness. Three times he decided he couldn't do this any more, but when he moved to get up, he suddenly felt even colder, and changed his mind. Where his shorts weren't close to his leg they'd gone stiff, like cardboard. He was trying to feel why, with his shivering fingers, when he realised his pants were frozen solid. His body stopped shivering, and went strangely still. He was feeling so cold he knew he was about to die. He had to go to the Home. It was too late for the breeze tube. His legs were so stiff it was hard to stand up, and painful to make them walk. So this was it, the end of him. All his life he'd worried about getting back to his sisters, but he might as well have died up in space, with Mum and Dad. He was squeezing out from between the shelter-shed and the fence, when he smelt his Mum's food. Shepherd's pie, hot, with potato on top, wafting over his thoughts. Plain food, but good for empty stomachs. His heart said 'thanks Mum', even though he knew his brain was playing tricks on him – it was all long ago. He sat down, his back against the shelter-shed wall, to think about that. It was a nice last thought. He looked at Dad's watch. The watch hands had stopped moving. They were frozen still, like he was. His thoughts stopped too. His head felt strangely empty. He was staring vacantly into the dark, when something got in the way. Some-one was standing over him. Putting something on the ground. Wrapping him in an old blanket. Holding a spoon in front of his mouth, like Mrs Benson had got him to do for the sick kitten at the Home.

'I'm glad you like it… I had to promise I wouldn't bring you home with me, but don't think we don't worry about you… All gone. You are a hungry little thing.'

The lady was gone away, swallowed by the darkness. He was full, and warm. He looked up through the clear night sky at the stars. Now he knew he must always remember: his life was a long journey, and if he just kept going, then one day, he would get up there. He just had to keep going. Mum and Dad weren't dead. They were waiting for him. They were out there somewhere among all those stars, hoping good hopes and thinking kind thoughts for him until they could be together again.

SERIOUS TROUBLE COMING, AND CADET CLUB IS CALLED PRETEND RUBBISH

Cadet Club was the best thing in his life. He had more homework from it than from school. Miss Shandy said he was too young to learn 'exact figures', but no-one was ever the wrong age to learn the ideas behind things. There were three basic Navigation techniques – by the stars, or by starting point in a pre-planned journey, or by internal relative motion sensing. While she swept floors and bucketwashed the toilet area, he would be stumbling around inside the hall, blindfolded, practising. Sometimes she would call out the positions of stars relative to him, other times she would call out speed to travel, for how long, or numbers of steps to take, before each direction change.

'Shield up voyager – it's cuppa time… We've come a long way, you and I. The first few nights you were here I couldn't trust you not to go wild on me with over-excitement. Watching watching watching all the time I was.'

'I'm good now, aren't I,' he said, carefully levering the lid off the hot chocolate powder tin.

'Good…' she said, thinking it over, 'I wouldn't say 'good' exactly, but at least, these days, you think before you do it.'

Not always – the thinking before he did things. It was the night before Space Day. Excitement everywhere. The parents were out the front chattering with Miss Shandy and the aeroplane pilot. Inside, he was the only kid who knew it wouldn't really be space, just up above the planet a bit. The others wouldn't believe him. They were making him feel bad, saying he was lying to ruin tomorrow. He didn't know where it came from, but suddenly the words splurted out of his mouth.

'We're not going in space, because you have to have a special haircut, and we haven't.'

It wasn't true as far as he knew – everyone's hair used to be just however it was at home on board, but he'd already said it. Then Dennis appeared with a big pair of scissors, and held them out.

'Show us.'

There was disagreement about who it should happen to.

'All right. I'll go first,' said Dennis, and now the game had changed from one, to fourteen haircuts.

He tried to do something interesting with the scissors that would look like a special haircut for something, but it didn't take long to realise that just getting hair off evenly, without making too much holes and stick-out bits, was hard enough. Everyone was

interested in progress. It was like a one boy race, with everyone
cheering him on, with whispers: 'Hurry, hurry,' until it was their
turn. Then the one having their hair cut would look thoughtful, as
they wondered about what was happening to their head. The
grade six boy was hard because he was tall. Snip snip, snip snip,
but it wouldn't look even, and there was no way of knowing what
the top looked like.

'Lefty, get up on a chair, or there won't be any hair left on
the sides.'
It took until supper to do everyone. James was last. Shane said,

'My Dad does it like that to the grass, if it's damp when
he mows.'
James had a weird spike sticking up crooked that the scissors
wouldn't cut. He was looking at his reflection in the office
window. He giggled, and said;

'Not me too! People don't go up in space looking stupider
than our dog! You fibbed, didn't you... You fibbed.'

'Yes.'
The word was hard to say, but he said it. He'd wanted to lie more
to hide the first one, but he'd had a sinking feeling just when his
mouth was opening, a bit like when he shut the escape pod lid for
his sisters, knowing he would be left behind.

'You're a bit of a stuffed unit, but we're friends', said
Shane.

 Dennis sniggered, like 'he he he'.

'I knew it was a bad thing,' he said, happy with the
thought.
The grade six boy was feeling his head. Joanne was trying to see
her reflection again.
Philip giggled, his eyes wildly excited,

'We are in so much trouble!'
Then they heard Miss Shandy say,

'Supper! Oh dear... suspiciously quiet in there'.

'Who did this? Who did this to my boy?... You, what's that little
one's name, the one with everyone's hair on him?... All right

Lefty, let's take you home and see what your parents have to say about this.'

The man was towering over him, powerful angry. He wanted to run, to hide, to get away from the fear. Fear that this would mean no more Cadet Club, and, no more school. Children who lived like animals behind sheds wouldn't be allowed near other children. He looked around, up at all the faces. He had no-one. No-one would help. Even Miss Shandy was looking like she was a far away separate life.

'Well? Where do you live?... Who knows where this boy lives?... Lefty, is it? Oh yes – now here's a pretty state of affairs…'

'He's staying with us, Alec. Children do these things…'

'Not to my boy they don't. Matthew's too old for this pretend rubbish. In the car.'

'It's only hair Dad.'

'In the car. We'll discuss this at home.'

Pretend rubbish. He thought about it while they drove to Shane's place. The words bit, sharp and hurtful into his heart. He had been hoping, really hard, all year, that Cadet Club's 'pretend rubbish' would get him back to his family. He had nothing else to give him hope.

'Lefty,…'

'His name's Mark, Dad.'

'Cadet Club isn't pretend rubbish. I want you boys to understand that. You are learning all sorts of things there, things that will get you out into life as healthy, capable adults. Apart from anything else, it is teaching you to be some-one other people will like to have in their lives. Anywhere you want to go, and anything you want to be when you get older – Miss Shandy is getting you ready for. She's a good lady, and your mother and I don't begrudge that coin each week, not the tiniest bit.'

This was that whole 'when you grow up' thing again. Mark looked out of the car at the night going past. Forgotten weedy grass tufts around worn-out houses, and sometimes between them a pocket view, into the dark empty distance. He was still too small, and Life was too big. A new quiet worn-out sadness was in him – he probably would get out into space – he might even find his family – but it was going to be a long, long journey, and he was getting scared that Mum and Dad would be old before he got there. In the background of his thoughts other thoughts were echoing. He wanted to make it home some time soon. Not just one day so far ahead in his life it didn't matter.

FINALLY, A HOME TO BE PART OF, AND A FAMILY TO SHARE BEING ALIVE WITH

Shane was really proud. Pushing open doors, dragging him through their house.

'This is our room.'

There wasn't much in it, and the things looked used, mostly a bit broken. There weren't beds, just a mattress on the floor.

'Sorry,' said Shane.

He meant for the mattress.

'We have to have an end each. Sorry.'

'Shane, it's okay. It's heaps better than a breeze tube mat.'

'Dad says the room's probably too small for beds anyway?' said Shane, brightening up again.

'Mum? He hasn't got any jarmies,' Shane yelled.

'Yes. Well, you decide which pair. And get a fresh towel out. I want our new family member washed. Lefty?'

Shane's mum appeared at the bedroom door.

'Now is a good time to start smelling like you live in a house.'

'Mum!'

There were adults talking at the front door. Shane's Dad saying thankyou.

'All right boys, out of the way. Bunk bed coming through.'

Later that night he was lying in bed with his stomach full of shepherd's pie again, looking at the wooden rail next to his face. It had Alan scratched into it. James's big brother. He wondered about how sometimes people knew more than you realised about you, but they minded their own business. The old mattress was leaning up against the wall. "For in case we have visitors over", Shane had said. Life was going to be better, so much better from now on.

SPACE DAY

Space Day was supposed to be like a fathers and sons, mothers and daughters day. After the hair cuts, things had changed. Joanne turned up with her dad, but everyone else came with their mums. As they waited for the bus to come he tried to look like he was sorry for what he'd done to everyone's hair, but inside, his heart was singing. He lived in a real house now, with a family. A family that liked having him around.

The plane went up, and up, until the colour started not being in the sky. The blue had gone off; dull, a bit like a bruise, on the way to being black. He could see out into space. The extensions that had come out of the wings earlier were wobbling, like there wasn't enough atmosphere to hold them up. The front of the plane did a shallow dive, then drifted its way up higher again. The pilot was watching all the gauges and indicators in front of him, like he had to see the slightest change the instant it happened. One wing dipped, and the plane tilted over, and then began to slide sideways. It felt horrible, like the pilot was only just managing to stay in control.

'Close enough to space?' he asked, without turning around.

'Yes thankyou,' they all said back.

'Good. Close enough for me too. That's the highest she's ever been.'

All the way down the mothers chatted. The other kids were fast asleep, lying all over their parents like floppy rag dolls. Mark stayed awake, watching everything that happened in the plane, so he would know more about getting away from a planet.

'Not sleeping?' asked the pilot.

'Like to fly her?... good lad. Wait for me before each thing to do, and I'll explain. The most important thing in this plane is no sudden corrections. If she drifts, drift her back, if she falls, let her, then work the controls bit by bit, for a gentle rise. Did you understand what I just said?'

'Yes.'

He flew the extreme altitude plane all by himself for ages, making steady corrections, and listening to the pilot's explanations of how to use the changing information the readouts were showing. He heard talk behind him. Bernard, awake.

'Lefty's flying us! Look, look!'

'Well done,' said the pilot, 'Your dad let you do something like this before?'

'Yes.'

'You're a lucky boy. I'd say you were nearly good enough to pass your Fly-ahead practical test, if we were on a planet that did that sort of thing. Now…see that cloud mass below us? That means some rough flying. Air pockets are going to bounce the Happy Flier around a bit. You go back to your seat, and strap yourself in.'

He nearly felt like his dad was with him in the plane, watching over him. Dad used to like it when he tried his best to do something properly. He giggled to himself about another memory of his father, when Dad was laughing and cranky at the same time: "Sometimes having fun just gets to come first, doesn't it Buster". Memories. He needed them, but they wouldn't get him through his future. The plane was flying inside a cloud. Ragged shadowy whiteness like his feelings. But hey, today wasn't bad. Today was good like his first night at Cadet Club, because he had finally seen a glimpse of space again, out there waiting for him.

He meant to ask Miss Shandy what a fly-ahead test was, but in the excitement of landing on solid ground again, and everyone talking lots before going home, he forgot.

LOSING A FRIEND, AND THEN LOSING EVERYTHING

He was in the Cadet Club gang now – Bernard, Philip, Dennis, Lefty, Shane, and James. Sometimes he felt it would be no time at all and they would fly in space together, not just him by himself to find his family, but all six of them in a team, like in "The Five Astrofighters of Stella islsea". It was good having friends. Then after a while he realised some-one had to come last, whatever they were doing, and it was nearly always James. If not James, then Shane. James would sook, and tell tales. Shane wouldn't talk to anyone and take his stuff back, if you were borrowing it. They were all sitting in class after lunch. Silent. Mark was just about to use the ruler on his drawing when Shane snatched it. Not to use, to put on the other side of the desk. Shane was really dark, because everyone had decided they'd had enough of James sooking on. Bernard and Philip said so. He looked across at James. James was red around the eyes, and white around the mouth. Having a big sook about being told he wasn't in the gang any more, because he was a sook. Well, he is, thought Mark, but his brain wouldn't let go of thinking about pushing James out of the lunch line. 'You're not with us – you lose – go to the back of the line' he'd said, and he'd felt strong and clever, at the time. Mark looked across at the ruler. He could just grab it. It wasn't like Shane was all that popular either. Bernard and Philip will side with me, he thought confidently.

'Touch it, and you can find some-one else's family to leach off,' said Shane quietly.

In that split fraction of a moment everything changed. Mark didn't want the ruler any more, because the drawing no longer mattered. School no longer mattered. He didn't want to be here. He didn't want to be anywhere. His hearing had gone funny, sort of humming buzzing in his head, when there was no humming or buzzing in the outside world to be heard. He saw his hand was shaking. He put it down on the desk, to keep it still. He knew he would never think of Shane's place as home again, not a real place you belonged home. This whole planet was suddenly strange and alien, far away from where-ever he should be. Not one person here was his family, not one thing here was from his home. A sharp, bitter pain was wrecking his heart. All along, he had been an outsider that they were being nice to for a while. He swung his head around to look out the window, to concentrate on things out there, until this went away. He felt angry, really sad, and inside he was hurting a lot. Scratching of pencils on paper went on in the background. The sound of Philip scrubbing at his picture with a rubber. Mr Arthurs' chair creaking as he reached around on his desk sorting things.

He sat, feeling off, far away, dead in his heart. I have to leave here. I have to get back out into space. I have to go ho… He couldn't think that word, because it made his eyes fill with water. Home, his family's space ship, was just wrecked broken rubbish, drifting away forever to nowhere. When today was over he would go back to Mrs Benson. To not enough food, to sharing a bed with littler kids who would cry all night, and to doing grown-up daily chores – dishes washing for heaps of people, clothes washing, including for the pukey pooey little kids, and scavenging and carting wood from the wrecked building sites around the children's Home. No more school. No more school lunches. No more bed of his own in a house with a family. No more gang of 'friends'. No more dreams of a future where he found his family. The afternoon dragged on, and on. The shadow from the sun slowly crossed the floor. Nearly time to say goodbye to this. He knew he was safe now – he wasn't going to cry, just feel a bit hard inside. He opened the desk lid and put the paper and pencils in. Closed it again, for the last time.

'You finished already?' asked Dennis from his desk. He had no answer. Dennis was just some-one he used to know until today. He heard a sneaky laugh.

'Shane's dissed Lefty.'

Bernard's voice. He knew he should hate the cunning chuckle that came after, but he didn't care any more. Shane passed the ruler back across the desk. Didn't say anything. Then Shane wiped one of his eyes. This deep unhappiness was like a spreading disease. Mr Arthurs was talking now;

'I will see all of you after school. The five grade four boys know who I'm talking about.'

MR ARTHURS DOES HIS VERY BEST

'Well… James should just toughen up.'

'Is that what you think, Bernard Avago,' said Mr Arthurs, 'So you're tough, are you? How about "Tough boys make mean men make an unhappy world", and then all of us have to live in it? You and Philip can go home with that thought in your heads. Don't forget it, because the pair of you will be writing it up on the board tomorrow. You other boys wait here while I call your parents.'

The door closed behind Mr Arthurs.

Silence.

Mark had no parents to be called, not on this world.

The classroom felt tired, empty, like a broken toy. He knew it was time to go. He'd finished being Lefty, forever. He took his single person rocket picture down from the pin up board. He lifted the school jumper down from the hook. No, it wasn't his to take. He put it back. Mrs Benson would find him something a bit warm.

'Sorry,' he said, mainly to James, but a bit to Shane.

Letting himself quietly out of the classroom door. Walking softly down the centre passage, past the lockers. He reached the double doors to the outside world, but they wouldn't open. He tried again, the handle making a soft sliding, scraping noise. He heard the floor creak behind him. Mr Arthurs. Mr Arthurs standing there, looking at the rocket picture.

'Not coming back then?' said Mr Arthurs softly.

'No.'

'That would be very sad for me. May I have one last look at your picture?'

He held it out. Mr Arthurs took it.

'I always liked this picture, because you are flying home to your family, and waving a happy goodbye to your friends. Who's that?'

'James.'

His eyes followed Mr Arthurs' finger across the painted paper. 'Shane.'

'So they have been good friends to you?'

He didn't know what to say. He looked along the row of lockers in the passageway, counting them pointlessly so he wouldn't think about things.

'Will you be saying a proper goodbye to them then?'

'No?' he said, feeling tortured.

'Good. Glad to hear it. Then this picture can go back up on our board. You had better take today's drawing home with you tonight, and get James and Shane to help, or it won't be ready in time. Didn't get a lot done on it today, did you?'

'No.'

Mr Arthurs was turning to walk back to the classroom, still talking.

'While you children are busy being children, wondering about how big life is, us grown-ups spend most of our time worrying about you, and whether our best will be good enough. We want, for all of you we want, happiness, and hopes, for you to know there is a place for you, and most important: we want you, as you grow up, to find lives you can enjoy living. I know you want to fly home Lefty, but where 'home' is for you is a bit beyond us at the moment.'

Mr Arthurs paused, thinking, a twinge of sadness blowing through his heart; the boy's mother and father would be spending every day of their lives terrified for this little creature's safety, worrying about where he might be, what might be happening to him. A school teacher could only do so much. Enquiries had gone in every direction, and they had all vanished into the forever echoing world of interplanetary communications. World by world they were spreading across the Universe, but no answers came back, just the echoing questions. No answer to what had happened to the boy's family. Ah well, tomorrow's film would brighten the boy up. It would be space, and adventure; the things the lad pined for, and also show a way a child could get up off a planet, and fly. Yes: get people's thoughts going in a positive direction again. Pin our hopes on that for now.

Mark was looking up at the man. Grown-ups never did anything, just stared at you while other things were happening in their head, and then just when you thought you should go, they would start talking again.

'Fly ahead now Lefty my lad, collect your friends, and I'll see you all tomorrow.'

THOUGHTS ABOUT FAMILY, AND NOISES IN THE NIGHT

As he and Shane and James walked home, he wondered about what had happened. Mr Arthurs hadn't made things right, or wrong, or better, just different, so life could go on. It wasn't clear why James was staying the night, but it felt safe that they were together, even though their problems were with each other. They reached that little rise in the road where it was level with the breeze tube. James chose a rock, picked it up, and threw. It went up, up, up… and over. First time ever.

'Yay!' squeaked James, more surprised than anyone.

'Let's quit while we're ahead,' said Shane dropping his stone.

His voice sounded like he knew things were going to be all right. Mark realised with surprise that someone was waving to him from inside the tube. Just a lifted hand, like "hello". It was the woman he ran into on his breeze mat, on his first day of school. He waved back happily, and then she was gone into her life again. She was someone else who felt lost and forgotten in the two vastnesses, the Great Universe, and all of Time. He did have family here. That was a funny thing: you could meet some-one only once and not even like them much but they were a bit family, and then, other people, you could like them a real lot, for a long time, but they would never be anything more than just someone else. I need my family, he thought. A lady who had kind thoughts for him that he sometimes saw in the breeze tube wasn't enough.

The blanket thing started to slide over the side of the bunk. He hauled it back up. His mind kept going over and over the day, every bad bit of it. He rolled his body over, and over again. That didn't help. It was his thoughts that were uncomfortable. The house was silent. Silent like it was empty. Empty of life. The night outside was so quiet he thought he could hear how big the planet was. Somewhere far away he heard a sound like the sky being torn, ripped apart by something going really fast. And then there was a dull, distant explosion, something crashing into the ground.

He sat up in his bunk.

'Did you hear that?"

The silent house swallowed his words. He lay there looking over the side of the bunk. James was half out of his sleeping bag, arms thrown wide, mouth open like he was singing in a choir.

Dreaming about something – his eyebrows kept moving up and down tiny amounts, like he was having a friendly understanding with someone. Shane's bunk was in blackness. There were no more distant noises outside in the night. He rolled over in his bunk again, and finally fell asleep.

A DAY HE WOULD NEVER FORGET

He woke up early. He could hear Shane sleeping in the bunk below. He could see James' sleeping bag on a mattress on the floor. It was curled up in a James inside it shape. Shane's mum was doing something quietly in the kitchen, early morning things she liked to get done: play lunches for schoolers, snacks for people who went to work, and sorting out fresh clothes for everyone. His own Mum used to do that. His own mum was still out there somewhere in the vastness of space. In the excitement of everything he'd been gradually forgetting his need to go home. I'm never going to forget again, he thought. Yesterday in the classroom was still fresh and hurtful inside him.

This world's sun was weakly backlighting the bedroom window's thin curtain. Soft early-morning colours were coming through it. Tomorrow had just become today, and it was going to be sunny. There were rummaging noises happening outside the bedroom – Shane's dad in the centre room picking things up, about to leave for work. Now they were speaking softly out there, Shane's parents, but from his place up on his bunk in the bedroom he could only hear one side of the conversation.

'Funny how Arthurs goes to so much trouble planning, and then, after all the petty officials and the money difficulties, it's the boys who nearly scupper everything with some petty squabble. June, don't expect well behaved boys home tonight – they will either be dog tired walking in their sleep almost, or vomiting cranky over-excited… Just making sure. This isn't the usual surprise Mothers' Club Day lollies and treats… Not for them anyway… Yes, Lefty particularly…'

The front door shut. Now there were just wiping benches noises from the kitchen.

'Shane. Shane. Wake up. What's mothers' club day?'
Shane sat up in his bunk like a light turned on.

'Ace – you like get to school, and there's… um… we get in a long line, and everyone gets a bag, with like some candy stuff, and party trick stuff, and um…, like last year, I got that model space ship in mine, and then we do games and stuff instead of lessons, or go on an excursion if it's… is it sunny? Oh ace. Ace!'

'Are you sure it's today?' asked James' head, as it appeared out the end of his sleeping bag.

'Real sure,' said Mark, but he wasn't sure that things were going to happen like Shane said, and a nasty fear began stalking him, jolting sharply into his thoughts each time he remembered Shane's dad's last words: "Lefty particularly". Something about today had more to do with him than anyone else, and knowing that didn't feel good. He knew what missing out felt like. His brain changed the subject.

'Hey? What's a fly-ahead test?'

He might as well ask; Shane might know, and sometimes James knew strange grown-up stuff from his big brother.

'It's when you go walk towards the window, coz there's this… buzzing sound… and you're thinking… flie ahead,' said Shane.

'This is going to be a pillow your head test,' yelled Mark, laughing and annoyed.

Annoyed because he'd been sucked into trying to figure out what Shane was on about.

'Enough in there. Up and dress yourselves.'

ON THE WAY TO SOMETHING BIG

'Boys, sit quiet and behave. We are not having another episode like on the breeze mats, are we.'

'No Mr Arthurs.'

There had been some mucking around on the breeze mats, which finished when Mark tried to jump Bernard and Shane lying on their mats, one after the other, and his mat tripped his feet. He had to somersault to stop himself, and everything ended up a noisy tangle of half the school blocking the breeze tube. Mr Arthurs had waded through the rest of the school to pick them up like puppies that had pooed the carpet. "The usual suspects won't be going to Funrides today, so keep yourselves near me, and behave, or you won't be going anywhere". Bernard muttered rude words, and James looked like he was going to cry. Mr Arthurs said it wasn't a punishment; they were going somewhere better. Not even James was believing him. Now they were on a bus, just the five of them and Mr Arthurs.

The travelacross bus looked familiar. So did the road they were going on, and then Mark just knew: airfield.

'I know where we're going,' he yelled.

Today was going to be good. They were all talking now, and twisting around on their seats to see, but they weren't there yet.

'Boys, don't get ahead of yourselves,' said Mr Arthurs. They stared at him, waiting for information. He began talking quietly to the bus driver.

'Twenty three years of teaching, and all I ever hear about is that ruddy plane. I went to school with Avro Kopter, and he was more grown up then than he is now. He lives for his once a year flight with Shandy's Cadet Club. Even more irresponsible than your average uncle. I called him to warn him the kids would be close by today, in case some pestering should happen, and he just says "Oh great, better stock up on candy".

'Where?' asked Mark loudly.

If not the high altitude plane, then where were they going? Mr Arthurs was turning around to face them.

'Who knows where the Spaceport tower is?'

'We're nowhere near there,' said Shane, like "you're not tricking me with childish stuff".

'Before the Spaceport tower we only had a Lifeworlds military base, and its airfield. These days anyone can use the hangars and what's left of the airfield's old runway, and the military base is now a Deep Space listening station. Now who would like to have another guess at where we're going?'

'There,' said Mark straight away, while Bernard was still getting "Deep Space listening station" ready in his head so he could say it right.

'And candy, at next door,' said James, looking happy and then embarrassed.

'Hmm,' said Mr Arthurs, 'the people in this military base are not used to grubby fingers collectives, so do your best to behave. One more thing: we aren't here for fun. Something important is happening out there in space, and we are lucky enough to be allowed in today to find out what. Now you know as much as I do, so off this bus, and we'll go inside that building and find out some more.'

INSIDE THE DEEP SPACE LISTENING OUTPOST, A FILM OF FEAR AND SADNESS, THAT LEAVES SOMETHING NEEDING TO BE DONE

Mark looked behind him. People in uniforms, and other grown-ups in those suits politicians wore. Grade Four extracted boys from Wastelands Primary School were the only children of any size.

'I'm an extracted Lefty,' he said, both shy and cheeky to Mr Arthurs.

'Yes, you are a real double hitter lad. Quiet now.'

He held onto his Mothers' Club Day bag and looked up at the blank screen, waiting. More talk. Not Mr Arthurs this time, but someone in a uniform out the front.

'Blue Skies One Space Outpost Outer 17 would like to welcome senior officials, military dignitaries, and community representations from the planet Outer 17.'

'That's us,' whispered Mr Arthurs, 'you boys are representing our community, so be good.'

'Welcome to our base for this special occasion. Today we are going to see an amazing film. It didn't come through any of the usual channels. It fell from space in a tiny capsule, sent by a ship in distress to warn everyone that something very unpleasant is out there. We are a Deep Space listening post, and it was in that role that we caught the tiny incoming distress message. So, what is so special? First you will see a freighter convoy being escorted by a Vervolf, a vicious heavily armed escort ship from a distant alliance called the Star Triangle. Small fast and powerful, these ships are often used in surprise attacks, but here the vervolf is escorting freight home. In this film we are going to see a new threat in space attack the convoy. The warning capsule was sent into space as the Vervolf lost ship after ship from its convoy, and eventually was fighting for its own survival. Its ship's boy sent this message to us from his Fly-ahead because we were the nearest planet. Even though the Star Triangle are hostile to us, the last thing in his life this boy did was send us this warning. We honour his memory today. A final point I need to mention: to those of us it concerns; the underlying issue of rescue or salvage sovereignty will be canvassed at the debriefing. For those entitled to vote time is running out for a decision. This is a very special film, sent to us at great cost. I would like you all to pay close attention to "He Died Alone Out in Space".

'Hmm,' said Mr Arthurs, like he didn't approve of the film's name.

The lights in the theatre dimmed. James, sitting next to Mark, said;

'I'm not watching if it gets scary.'

The screen's dull fuzziness was sharpening into a view of a passageway inside a ship. Someone was walking in it, but you couldn't see them, because the camera making the images was mounted on them somehow. Hands came up and lifted the camera off a boy's head – he was looking into the lens now. He was a relaxed, pleased with himself boy. A boy that is probably going to die before the end of this film thought Mark. He sat in his theatre seat unhappily wondering about that.

'Today is my first time at the controls of a real whole big ship,' the boy was announcing just for the camera to hear, 'and this is my film of it'.

Walking in through a bulkhead hatchway onto the bridge control centre of some large vessel. Putting his cap on something just inside the door, and pointing it towards a seat to one side of the bridge that had 'backup helmsman' written on the back of it. The camera was picking up sounds on the control bridge, mostly people talking in the background.

'Unexplained problems with the second freighter's forward shield Sir?'

'More detail.'

'It has been working loose from the hull for no observable reason.'

'Thankyou Fourth. Have freighter 265 drop back four places in the queue. Comms one keep me informed of developments.'

'Yes Sir.'

'We seem to be alone, but unexplained maintenance problems used to be the first sign of a skulking unwelcome presence: low level aggressive sabotage as a diversionary tactic, before an attack. Highly unlikely way out here, but perhaps we will make the most of this, and look upon it as an exercise. Wait for my order.'

'Yes Sir.'

'Fly-ahead's here Sir, for his reward for staying out of trouble three whole days in a row… A record for him Sir.'

'Very well Third, have him replace the main helmsman.'

The boy turned around at the words, and came back to re-aim the camera at the central seat on the bridge, his face embarrassed pleased. Boring normal stuff, just another boy somewhere else being a boy, which reminded Mark he had something to do.

'Boo!' he said suddenly into James' ear.

'Ha ha very funny,' said James, and then Mark felt Mr Arthurs' hand on his head, aiming it back at the screen.

Mark was interested in the ship's controls, and in particular, how would a boy get to steer them? The boy stood where he was told in front of the large helmsman's seat, took hold of one end of the hand controls bar, something went beep beep beep, and the hand control bar telescoped into itself until he could reach the other end too, and when the boy had both handles gripped tight the seat shrank in and then moved up behind him. He wriggled himself onto it and waited.

'When you are sure you are ready, you hold your left hand up… yes, into the invisible beam, and you've now claimed control of the vessel.'

'But I can't see anything?'

'This isn't a fly-ahead, boy. You're not sitting in your own little cockpit now. Bridge width visuals for the helmsman please Fourth, and then adjust his targeted gravity centre. We don't want your arms and legs flailing around all over the place the first move you make, do we.'

'No Sir, but I don't know what that means?'

'You and the ship are now one weight. No matter how quickly it turns or stops or accelerates, to you it will be as if you are both standing still, and it is the Universe turning and tilting around you.'

Silence on the bridge. Two long lines of freighter hulls stretching out in front, with a clear space up the middle for the Vervolf to move back and forth between them. Beyond the freighters was blackness carpeted with stars. Peaceful, everything in order.

'Helmsman, take us up to the front of the convoy. I want an explanation for that faulty freighter. Third, we will begin the exercise now: have the off crew rise and man all stations: for the purpose of this exercise we are anticipating hostile intent.'

'Yes Sir.'

'When do I say my "yes Sir",' asked the boy.

'Straight after your order, so the captain knows you have understood.'

'But I didn't know he'd finished talking to me.'

'Concentrate on obeying the order now Cort, or you will miss your turn.'

'Yes Sir.'

'Weapons are clear of the hull skin, locked and loading, charging, and preheating. All armour segments register as sealed.'

'Thankyou in-hull comms. Route all ready-state message board outputs to the tactics table.'

'Yes Sir.'

'We are a very powerful ship, aren't we.'

'Yes boy. The Ray of Fire 4 is the best armed and the fastest ship of its size. A vessel to be proud of.'

Silence on the control bridge. The Ray of Fire was moving up between the freighters, steered by the fly-ahead boy. He was so tiny with everything big around him, but he was in control of it all. A freighter that had been up near the front was dropping back past the other freighters, to where a gap in the line was being made for it. Mark was just thinking the large viewing screen across the Ray of Fire's bridge wasn't very good quality when the boy spoke up again.

'Scuse me? But why do the stars look so flat and close up? Is that right?'

The boy sounded doubtful. There was silence for a moment, then:

'Get that boy off the bridge. Exercise cancelled. Sound battle stations. Engage entire power train. Lock down for action. Prepare to engage an unknown enemy.'

People were yelling 'Sir' everywhere on the control bridge, muttering into headsets, and flicking switches quickly above them and in front of them. Alarms were hooting, the lighting in the passageway outside was going off and on like a warning, and more ship's crew were running in through the bulkhead hatchway, belting themselves into seats, and turning console screens on. The boy was standing out of the way just inside the hatchway, waiting for his chance to get out.

'Right Boy – run down and check your Fly-ahead is securely locked to the deck, and then go to your battle station.'

'Yes Sir.'

The boy was off the control bridge. His hat was back on but the image was hard to follow because the Ray of Fire had begun to move around, causing the boy to stagger as he ran, into the sides of the passage, sometimes flat on his face on the floor, and now suddenly bouncing off the deck above his head.

'We are firing at something already,' said the boy to himself, sounding surprised.

He was determined to get wherever he was going, picking himself back up after falling only to be sent flying down the passage with his feet unable to grip the floor as the ship around him surged forwards, engines roaring, weapons making strange charging sounds, and machinery all through the ship doing weird flat-out noises. The boy had reached a hatch and was trying to get over the coaming so he could climb down the ladder beneath it, but he couldn't get his balance. He had one leg over, a foot reaching frantically for the top ladder rung, when the Ray of Fire lurched and the boy fell in and down head first. There was a noise of ladder rungs being bashed into and then the boy was back up the right way, just in time because Mark had started to feel like he was going to be sick, from watching all the off balance images from the head camera. The boy's voice called out in a crying whimper;

'I broke my finger.'

The ship jolted harshly and the boy's hat smacked into the ladder, with a safety helmet hitting the road sound, and he dropped down two more rungs. He seemed to be refocused by that, and now he was on the move again, reaching the bottom of the ladder, bouncing up off the deck below, landing again crooked but on both feet, and then running flat out across the deck as everything tilted away from beneath him. He was crossing an equipment storage area, sprinting towards a small flying craft no bigger than a small terrestrial car, but it was sliding around too, dangerously, and twice the boy had to turn and run away or he would have been knocked down and squashed. The third time the Ray of Fire tilted and the craft began to slide the boy was nearly there. He hesitated, bouncing nervously on his toes, deciding whether to wait for it to reach him and jump onto it, or run. Jump, thought Mark, jump: don't waste the chance, but then the craft began to pick up speed, sliding across the deck with screeching and grating noises. It looked strangely threatening, big and heavy enough to smash a jumping boy into broken bones. No, don't do it, panicked Mark changing his mind; run. Run. Mark could tell this time the boy was too slow. The helmet camera was looking the other way down the equipment storage area as the boy ran, but Mark could hear the screeching of the craft's skids as it came up behind. The bulkhead loomed large in front of the boy. There was nowhere left to run: he was going to be squashed into a bloody broken mess. James squeaked in the next theatre seat, and hid his head between his knees. At the last second the boy jumped high and towards the bulkhead, hands and legs extended to spring back from it. He was in mid air when the Ray of Fire lurched, bringing the bulkhead suddenly closer. The boy smacked into it like an insect into a window, and then fell onto the little craft below him as it rebounded back out into the equipment area. He had landed sideways, head down into the open cockpit, legs in the air. The little craft slid around pointlessly now, uncontrolled, bashing into stored machinery. The boy's legs were waving like two small branches in a wind; the boy was dead or unconscious.

The legs began to move, wriggling the boy right way up and down into the craft. He was slamming the cockpit cover above his head, strapping himself in, flicking switches, and suddenly everything changed; now the boy was in control.

'My ship: my rules,' he squeaked, like he was telling the Universe to behave.

'Ouw?' he added as an afterthought, and brought his hand up to his mouth to suck it.

Outside the little craft the Ray of Fire was still moving in all directions, but the boy was flying a more even middle course, only occasionally touching on the deck or the roof of the hangar space, and keeping clear of the bulkheads. He kept fiddling with one set of knobs and switches while he flew, but always got the same answer:

'Hangar anchorage not engaged. Your onboard system is damaged. Unable to lock down your craft. If your craft is not locked down it must be ejected. You must request assistance.'

Over and over came the automated warnings as the boy tried adjusting all sorts of things. A blinding red light was flashing now. One side of the equipment store became wide open to the blackness of space, and all of a sudden the little fly-ahead craft was out in the dark, on its own.

'No. No,' said James to himself, 'something bad will get you.'

The little craft was keeping close to the large bulk of the Vervolf, so close Mark couldn't see what was happening out front. Tucked in beside the larger craft looked like the only safe place to be, because twisted bits of wreckage kept hurtling past. Suddenly the Fly-ahead was thrown upside down and away by a huge orange light being shot out from one of the Ray of Fire's weapons. Over and over the little craft tumbled while the boy watched everything around him.

'Why doesn't he do something?' wondered Mark out loud.

'The little plane thing's all broken already,' decided James.

'I'm being a piece of wreckage while I find out what's going on, so I don't get targeted,' said the boy in the little craft to himself, like he was repeating his version of a lesson he'd been taught. Now the Fly-ahead had drifted far enough out of the Ray of Fire's shadow that the view in front could be seen by the helmet camera. Robotic ships with huge dangly legs were flying into the convoy and wrapping themselves around the freighter hulls. When the freighters tried to stop themselves being carried away, paddles came out of the huge legs to steer the power from the freighters' engines, so the freighters' motors would just make things worse for them. The Ray of Fire was blasting the robot ships to pieces, shattering them off the freighters, but even as one set of huge legs were blown to pieces more robot ships would speed up out of the darkness and start grappling onto the convoy. The wreckage of a large leg was drifting past. The boy righted the little craft and flew quickly inside its twisted broken shell, then found himself a hole in it to put the nose of the little craft at, so he could look out. There was at least one mother ship out in the blackness somewhere that was launching weapons. Weapons that were creeping around in the dark, then suddenly bursting into rocketing redness and bashing into the vervolf's hull. They didn't seem to be doing any damage. The Ray of Fire would just rock a bit, and then blast more of those freighter grabbing things to pieces.

'Oh,' said the boy like he had just thought of something, and then he flicked a few switches, and began adjusting two dials.

A garbled buzzy version of voices came out of a little speaker. It sounded jagged, and didn't make sense. The boy bashed the console in front of him.

'Properly,' he demanded, 'break their code properly', then he said 'please?'

He tweaked the other knob, and the Ray of Fire's bridge signal came through.

'I don't know how, but Cort's out there Sir. I can see the fly-ahead's tail navigation light reflecting off that weckage.'

'I can't open the hull. I'm sorry. I can't have the hull open until this is over. Tell him to turn his damn light off and stay hidden, and not to reply: they'll lock onto his signal.'

'Yes Sir. Light just went out.'

'At least he's listening for a change. Take over comms with the Fly-ahead Third. Dedicate a channel to him. We have flown into the middle of something big. Tough as we are, we are only one small ship, and we are going to go down. We must get a message out, and the boy is our best chance. That boy is our only chance.'

In the cockpit of the Fly-ahead the jagged speaker had suddenly gone clear: voices were coming in packets of sound as the decoder dealt with the signal:

"They're outcalling to something. Whatever it is, get it… Sweep for a return signal… suspect wreckage first. No message must get out. … Loss threshold exceeded: over three hundred collector drones irretrievable. Three hundred two, three… …new priority regime: Prohibit at any risk all outward signals, all message torpedoes, all escape craft. Launch dual fighter units. Vaporize rescue pods when they appear. Nothing must leave. Secondary objective; bring down that vervolf; divert all collector drones to that task. Bury it in collector drones until it is immobilized. Destroy remaining freighters: cargo collection is no longer our priority. All docking stations and pontoon factory units close down as of now: we will cleansweep and relocate inside three hours."

The signal from the vervolf bridge began coming in over the top of the decoder voices. The boy turned his attention to it.

'We have a position for the mother ship Sir.'

'Take us to it and we'll take it down with us, Fourth. Right up close. I want to see the whites of their eyes. I'm not blowing us all out of existence for a decoy signal… Repeat your comment Engines?… …Understood. Good suggestion: Third, tell the boy to wait for our Last Light, and then ride the shockwall. If he surfs the debris he should get clear space to launch the distress signal from.'

'Yes Sir.'

'And tell him to try adjusting his decoder. Anything searching for him will be on a localized signal, and he'll want to hear them coming.'

'Yes Sir. Cort, I'll repeat the bridge conversation in case you missed it.'

The boy was listening to instructions from the vervolf's third officer while he made adjustments to the decoder, then unclipped things from around his cockpit, fitting them onto mountings and into couplings alongside his seat. All the time he was watching what was happening outside his little craft. Dual crew fighter craft were cruising around in the wreckage now, and stabbing weapon rays into anything large enough to hide a fighterflier in. They were working their way steadily closer. And closer. The boy suddenly steered the Fly-ahead out of hiding, and then inside a smaller piece of wreckage.

'Wow! Good flying,' said Mark, without realising he was talking out loud.

The boy waited in his new hiding placed, tensed, but no purple ray came to burn his little ship, and him. He poked the little craft's nose forward into the tangled mess of the wreckage until he could see out again. Now the vervolf was hidden somewhere inside a mass of those long legged drones, and more and more were joining the ugly ball of death they were making for the ship and crew inside. The boy's hand came up near the camera to wipe his eyes, and he sniffed, but his voice wasn't crying when he spoke.

'My best weapons,' he said into the silence between the Third officer's sentences, as he stroked a barrel he'd just fitted next to his seat that had "marker paint sprayer" on it, then patted the equipment he had connected up on the other side of his seat, "Plate repair glue dispenser".

The Ray of Fire had flown away into the distance, taking its cocoon of tangled giant robotic legs with it. Red glows would happen, and bits of legs would be blown off the ball. The vervolf was still fighting somewhere inside, still blasting things apart. The dual crew fighters turned back to follow the ugly mess, shooting at anything that flew free into space.

'That's only five. Only five went. Keep watching out,' James was saying to himself in a worried whisper, as if he was willing the Fly-ahead boy to hear.

'Five what?' asked Bernard.

'Dual fighters,' said Shane, 'one of...'

'Shh,' said Mr Arthurs.

The Fly-ahead seemed to be alone, with only rolling and tumbling wreckage around it for company. Third's signal was still coming through from the distant vervolf.

'You are a good boy, Cort. We are all proud you were on our ship. We know you will do your best. We won't be going home for a while, so you need to get that message through for us... Where we're going next we won't be able to come back for you, not in time, so like I said – get as far away from here as you can before you launch your distress signal. Someone might pick you up. It has happened. While you are still alive, don't give up hope. Don't ever give up hope... If you make it away from here, turn your heating down – it will get you an extra day or two's power for life support. I have to go now – we are nearly ready to explode the outer hull. Just as well too – she's getting very sluggish on the helm. Remember: a little white light first, and then a brilliant shock wall, and you fly like a mad thing, away to better days. Bye kid.'

There was a shadow moving across the wreckage the little Fly-ahead was hidden in. Slowly, sneakily, something was getting very close. Creeping up from behind. The shadow fell across the Fly-ahead's control console, and now the boy Cort's hands moved just as stealthily, to the marker paint sprayer, to pressurize it. His hands went back onto the helm control.

'Ready, set,' he whispered, and the Fly-ahead suddenly flicked around to face the other way. Nothing there at the hole in the wreckage that he had to escape out through, not yet. The decoder began talking again.

'You can break comms silence to us, boys. There's movement: he knows we're here. My guess is it's a fly-ahead: wonder-kid in a toy ship that they send to scout out ahead. He's going to die anyway, so – how about a little sport?'

'Flush him out and we'll soft weapon hit him around a bit, like kick to kick.'

'Yeah, but wait 'til we get there.'

'Won't be much fun. By the third or fourth hit he'll be like a rat caught in a high pressure hose strainer; muscles coming away from his bones.'

'And sockets tearing open as his arms and legs come out. We need to set a power limit, so he gets a chance to give us a decent game.'

'It's not like he isn't going to die anyway.'

While the crews were talking between themselves, organizing their 'game', the nose of a dual fighter appeared, moving slowly across the Fly-ahead's way out of its wreckage hiding place. The boy inched the little craft forward, and then softly rolled the switch of the marker paint sprayer to on. A mist of white marker paint came out, then a gentle spray of droplets, streaming steadily away from the Fly-ahead's nose until they landed on the hull of the dual fighter.

'Ooouw? That's not much of a weapon,' whined Bernard, making Mark look across the seat row.

James was crouching down so only his eyes and the top of his head looked out over the seat in front. Mr Arthur's hand again, turning Mark's head back to the screen. More comms talk was happening.

'Any second now I'll be looking into his scared little face, so you lot better hurry; he might try making a break for freedom.'

'Hey come on: that's not fair. Lewis, tell Dean that's not fair: we can't see where you are for wreckage. There's like a rolling forest of broken stuff between us and you.'

'Yeah: wait for us.'

'We are waiting. I'll turn the sensors up to the max; he might be talking to himself like that scout we fried last week.'

'That was funny as: whispering all that bravado crap to himself about how we're going to be toast, when it's like twenty of us to one of him, and then he's like squealing in pain and begging us.'

'It wasn't funny. It was friggin awful. You're an arsehole Sinarter.'

'Hey… I was only saying it coz that's how we're supposed to feel! You know – tough like.'

'Well don't. I'm not up for that game of hit to hit any more. It's just some terrified kid who could have had a better life if we hadn't come along.'

'Yeah. You finish him Dean. Like now. See you back on board. By the way Lewis, your voice comms need adjusting: they've got an echo.'

The dual fighter with the Lewis and Dean voices was still moving steadily across the hidy hole opening, and changing from armour grey to marker paint white as it went. The paint spluttered.

'Don't run out don't run out,' whined the boy softly, and then he tapped the paint canister gently with a finger, until the paint stream firing out the front of the Fly-ahead became even again.

His leg was shivering. Not all the time, just in sudden starts.

'He's scared,' whispered Philip.

'He's not scared. He just needs a pee,' said James.

'Good one Chicken Boy – just needs a pee,' commented Bernard with half a giggle.

Philip started to say something, but Mr Arthurs interrupted him.

'Shush all of you.'

'Mr Arthurs, I didn't say anything yet?' said Mark, thinking it was funny because he was getting away with saying something.

'Most amusing Lefty, now be quiet.'

'You have to last until you've covered their sensor arrays,' Cort was whispering to the paint dispenser.

Voices were coming out of the Fly-ahead's speaker again.

'Bloody hell. These new fighters are crap. I shouldn't have turned the array up: the whole lot's gone down now. We're going to need a tow back. Serious. We can't see where we're going even, it's like all gone down, and they don't have like a cockpit real view any more even, because of the new armour. Woah! Junk's beginning to knock us around. Hey? Anybody left out there?... Oh good one.'

'Keep your hair on. We're still here. Have you got no outside information at all? Except low level, like just voice comm I mean.'

'Yeah. We can't see a bloody thing, and we've got no idea what we're flying into.'

'Stay still then.'

'Oh yeah, as if: all of us, everything here, it's all going like a thousand miles a minute across space compared to the nearest star belt, and all the wreckage is dancing around all over the place like some crazy shoot-em-up game, we can't see a bloody thing and stuff is bashing into us all the time, and you go "oh just stay still then righty ho". Ha ha. Get a tow line to us.'

While all the talk was going on the boy Cort had been edging the Fly-ahead out of its hiding place, ready to fly for his life through the mass of tumbling wreckage, hoping to escape into clear space.

'I meant stay still because we don't want to lose where the target is.'

The boy paused, uncertain, at the mouth of the hole in the wreckage, just behind the tail of the dual fighter.

'We see you now. Sinarter and Libbo will tow you back. We'll wait here and give the kid a chance.'

Cort backed the Fly-ahead into hiding again.

'He has to die, Waller.'

'Yeah yeah, but he might as well think he's about to escape. One last run. Not such a bad way to die – thinking you've made it... He's in one of these pieces of junk?'

Another fighter appeared, cruising like a shark among the tumbling forest of passing wreckage.

'Don't suppose you can tell us which one? Dean? Lewis?... Talking to ourselves. We'll park here until he makes a move.'

The boy sighed a sad, scared, giving up whine. The fighter was parking right in front of his hidey hole, too close to sneak away from, and just far enough away to have room to manoeuvre to train weapons on him as he ran. The fighter was turning slowly as it scanned the surrounding wreckage, looking for a little hidden space ship small enough to have just one boy inside. The fighter began frying lumps of wreckage as they went past, with some small ray weapon. They were probably bored. The boy was trying to pee into a clear hose, but his hand kept shivering. Big relieved sigh. Stopper into the tube, tube tucked back in its stowing slot.

'Now for number two,' he said, as he folded out a handle on the panel repair glue canister, and began to wind it.

Snapped it back down into place. A nozzle like a weapon barrel had appeared at the front of the Fly-ahead. The boy wiggled a stick inside, and the barrel wiggled out there in response.

'Umm,' said the boy thoughtfully.

He had a weapon of sorts, but what could he do with it? The fighter's front was swinging around closer and closer. Soon it would be looking straight into this wreckage at the Fly-ahead, and then everything would be over. Small bits of wreckage kept hitting the fighter on their way past, like leaves in wind hitting a parked terrestrial vehicle, then a large lump of passing wreckage hit the fighter, knocking it sideways and away a little bit.

'I wish they'd stop doing that,' said an annoyed voice, as the fighter went back to its search position, 'it's like rattle rattle like rain drops or something, and then just when you're not expecting it: biffo, and I have to reset everything.'

'I wish they'd do it more,' whispered the boy to himself. Suddenly his hand was on the aiming stick, swinging the glue barrel around frantically, aiming at the passing wreckage, and shooting globs of glue off. The glue balls traced lazy paths through the empty spaces between the wreckage until they hit a target, and began to chemically bond to the surface. Now he waited, watching, as the first pieces of wreckage reached the fighter's hull. One bounced off. One missed altogether. Another one bounced off.

'You're supposed to glue hull plates together – so glue!' he said, sounding both surprised and disappointed.

Another one missed... and one stuck. Two. Three. Yes! He did have a weapon, but could it do enough? The fighter was nearly aimed right at him. They must see him soon.

'What are we now, a flippin magnet?... No, it's just that all the crap going past is like sticking to us! Look! Crap coming to us, and, swing the viewer around, and... nothing. Just an empty hole in all the crap after us.'

'Hull surface checking camera: get it running... Oh shit. Shit. That little crap head's got us covered in plate repair glue. Shoot. Just shoot! Everything! Any more of this and we won't be able to fire without damage to us. I mean from the back blasts off all this crap we've got stuck on. If it gets over the steering nozzles we'll really be stuffed. No wonder Dean's sensors went down.'

'He won't be dead upstream: that would be too obvious – I'll swing us around and you take out every piece of garbage larger than a shit tin. Do it. Do it!'

'Yeah, all right! The mini zapper won't aim. It's like jammed on something.'

'The bloody hull cannon will. I'm swinging us around, you turn it on. We're taking out everything. Little prick, and to think I didn't want him to suffer.'

The boy was working hard, aiming and firing glue globs frantically at everything that went past. This side of the fighter was looking like some sort of fancy biscuit covered in chocolate shavings. A whole leg section of one of those freighter-stealing things rolled past and stuck onto the fighter's hull, like a huge tail. Cort giggled. And then the fighter's hull cannon turned on. It was a big purple search-light that turned everything in its path a brilliant burning blue and then shattered it into billions of tiny bright pieces. Not just the first thing it touched on, but everything it lit up, all the way into the dark distance.

'Five minutes of cannon power left: he's not going to get very far.'

'Yeah! That one. That piece there! You can see like a trail of tiny blobs coming from it. Swing us around, swing us around. He's fried!'

'Hang on. She's steering like a piece of poo right now. Just hold your horses; it's not like he can go anywhere.'

The boy's hand left the gluer's controls. He spoke, his voice sounding very different, like all the fun of his life had left, and only the feelings in his saddened heart remained with him.

'I'm going to die now,' he said quietly.

He looked down. Pulled his space suit zipper up all the way. Tightened his helmet strap.

'I flew a real ship today,' he said, remembering something good from his life.

He put his hands firmly on the helm controls. The purple of the cannon ray began to lick the side of his piece of wreckage. He crouched forwards. He spun the Fly-ahead's little motor up to full revs. A faint white light began shining from behind him, like the last light on a dull winter's day.

'Poor little bugger's fucked now anyway: there goes his mother ship. They still do that Last Light thing. All right, let's ray cannon the crap out of his sorry sad little arse.'

The Fly-ahead shot forward with a razor-sharp zing, the boy immediately swerving wildly through the sea of wreckage. Up down left left left right roll over left hard right flat out into a gap, through it, darting back into cover and dodging around again, all the time trying to get going faster, the Fly-ahead's little motor screaming. The purple ray swept across space and was suddenly nearly on him. He panicked, and lost control, hitting a broken piece of armour plate that sent the little Fly-ahead spinning off in a new direction, back into the wreckage shadows. The jungle of wreckage seemed to have no end. Blue light was shining brilliantly everywhere behind him. Shattered debri was rattling into the back of the little craft and shooting past in showering sparks. The bouncing around and mad swerves of the Fly-ahead were making Mark feel sick. There was saliva dribbling in a trail from the boy's mouth, and then the boy threw up, the vomit floating around inside the cockpit in sprays of bubbles. He was steering and working the accelerating thing one handed, while he wiped his other hand across his mouth.

'Fly, don't cry. Fly, don't cry,' he was saying over and over to himself as he wrenched the Fly-ahead's controls around. He was finally at the edge, the outer expanding edge of all the battle debris the Ray of Fire had made destroying those things with legs. Clear space, but the dual fighter would still find him out here. Now he flew straight, out into the darkness, leaning forwards hard over the controls as if that would help to go faster. He screamed a terrified squeak as all of space suddenly went bright orange behind him, but the Fly-ahead was still flying. There was a rattling sound at the back of the little ship, like big hail stones on a roof, and wreckage began to race past him again. Wreckage lit up orange from a massive explosion. A huge wall of wreckage, like it was a shock wave of broken metals. The Ray of Fire 4 had exploded its engines and was no more.

'Go go go,' the boy willed the little craft.

Bigger lumps were hurtling past. One nudged him, pulling him sideways and off course. He fought the little craft around again, and back up to maximum power. The dual fighter suddenly shot past him, its solid fuel hull-sacrifice escape rockets roaring. The stuck on wreckage was glowing orange. The comms decoder began talking again.

'How did they do that? It was only one of those tiny Star Triangle vervolf things, and it's breeched the Glory of the Universe's captive magma dams. Boy are we toast. Now I feel homesick.'

The dual fighter flew on, vanishing into the dark. The boy was still leaning over his controls, and now rocking in his seat to help his little craft ride the solid wave of superheated speeding wreckage that was pushing him on faster and faster out into empty space. Cold, empty, lonely space.

'Uh-oh,' said Philip.

'Mr Arthurs? He has to find a planet, doesn't he, because they don't give him enough air in his ship,' said Shane, worried for the boy.

'Quiet boys.'

The Fly-ahead was flying steadier now, just ahead of the huge wall of wreckage. Cort was setting things on its dashboard. He shivered, and turned something back up. Then down again. Now he was setting a predetermined course for the little ship to keep flying on. Finished that. He pulled a white sausage shaped capsule out from somewhere behind him, and opened a door in it. There was room to put something inside. The head helmet was coming off. The camera was being unmounted. Hand-held to focus back on his face. His eyes looked deep into the lens, as if Cort knew he was talking to the people in the theatre.

'I'm sending this so you can save your worlds from something very bad. Tell my mum I did like she said? I was good, most of the time I was. Third said... Third said they were proud of m...'

The boy couldn't finish because his voice went up tight; he was crying inside, and then the camera went off.

Dead silence in the theatre. Waiting. Was the man supposed to come out the front again, before people stood up from their seats? No, the film wasn't over: the screen was filling with an image again: the boy. The camera was being taken back out of the message torpedo. Time had gone by. The skin around the sides of his mouth was yellowy green tinged, but the rest of him looked bluish, and every few moments he was doing big shuddering shivers. He began talking in tight little half spoken whispers, like in a dream.

'You can save me. I'll show you. I'll show you, and then you can save me.'

The camera was being pointed at the control dashboard of the little ship, starting over on the left.

'This is how much air and cleaned water I've got. And how much coldness. And these ones in the middle are how fast, and where I'm heading. Oh... you can't see your solar star because my cockpit glass clamps it down to background light level. Anything big that doesn't change, the glass can do that. Third says that's so I don't get cooked. Right now I'd like to get cooked a bit... a lot even. Umm. I don't know what these ones on the right side are, much. They never come on before. I think it's things shutting down. Things that probably aren't needed if the motors are off. I haven't run out of power – I have to be really quiet.'

The camera was doing sudden shakes as the boy's hand, holding it, shivered. It swung around to Cort's face. He looked straight into the lens, his eyes tortured with sadness, panic, and fear.

'Please come and get me.'

The message torpedo lay there open and ready, but Cort wasn't putting the camera in. He seemed to have forgotten it was in his hand. It was pointed at a spray of frozen vomit on the cockpit ceiling. The boy was looking at the part of the control console he didn't understand.

'I'm not alone. There's something out there. I can't send the message. There's something out there.'

Mark felt a jolt of fear: an unexpected voice was coming from immediately behind him in the theatre.

'He's lost it. Going delusional.'

'That's the trouble with kids: always in their own play world, and when the chips are down, well – unreliable. He thinks there's something out there, so the life saving message never leaves: sentencing himself to death.'

Conversation had broken out among the adults in the theatre, discussing the boy's actions.

'If you checked his gauges – that one he held his finger under, as if that would help him understand it, was the proximity register: and it was saying nothing out there larger than an oversize rubbish bin.'

'Well, if you checked his gauges there was enough power there to run whatever engine he's got for a week at least, and he's got it off: freezing himself to death early.'

'No; the engine's off so the bogey man out there won't hear him.'

'Hopeless: as if flying silent is going to save him from his imagination.'

'Could we have less discussion in the theatre please. If there is time there will be a discussion component in the debriefing.'

Cort had clipped the camera back onto his flight helmet. He was getting a long skinny tube tin out of a side locker. Pulling its crossthreaded end off. Tipping out the contents. Half eaten bag of lollies. Very old looking packet of chips.

Munching noises happened while he packed the tube with frozen pieces of vomit collected from around the cockpit. End screwed back onto the container properly this time. The message torpedo was lifted out of its cradle. In went the container. The cradle was shoved forwards into a hole. The cover snapped shut. Cort's finger was poised over push buttons, while he thought.

'I need engines… no, just power to the launcher.'

Thinking again, with nothing happening in the little cockpit.

'I have to turn the engines on after I've launched the decoy. One little circuit coming to life shouldn't matter?'

Cort clicked two switches above his head, tiny lights came on in a few places around the cockpit, and then he pressed a push button on the torpedo launcher cover. A hissing sound, and the container was shooting away from the little craft, out ahead in the darkness, towards distant stars. It buckled, bulged, and the back end suddenly shot off, frozen sick shooting out like booster rocket flames. And that was as far as it got. A needle width size purple ray came out of the darkness, and the container was briefly a fizz of brilliant blue whiteness, and then it was gone. Now Cort was angling his head to look up and sideways outside. There it was, a rubbish bin sized drone with a tiny ray gun mounted on it, flying along parallel to the Fly-ahead.

'So… I haven't got any weapons to get rid of you, and you haven't got enough power to stop something as big as a Fly-ahead…'

Cort turned his attention to the walls of the cockpit. Looking, looking. Behind his seat was another launcher like the one for the message torpedo, only it was a bit larger, and it had a storage box next to it. He opened the lid and a voice started immediately from a little player stuck to the inside.

'Cort, shut the lid. I've told you your Fly-ahead is not a play thing. You are not to fool around with the mines.'

The boy half shut the lid, glancing around as he did so because something had moved in the corner of his vision. Beyond the reflections in the cockpit windows of everything in the cockpit the drone was out there, moving in closer. He opened the lid again. Unclipped a ball shaped thing a bit big to hold in his hand. Glanced around again. The drone's miniature ray gun was swinging slowly around to aim into the cockpit.

'Um um um, three seconds? One to fit it in, one to launch it, one to put on my shock restraint harness?'

He looked around again. The drone was moving in close, the ray weapon aimed into the cockpit, straight at the boy.

'Ohw!' he said, sounding indecisive, worried, and panicky.

'It doesn't begin the count until after it fires, so how long?' he wailed.

He suddenly adjusted something on the ball, slammed it into the launcher, rammed the launcher home, pressed its go button, threw himself down into his pilot seat, and squeezed the accelerator trigger until his hand went white. The purple ray was shining through the cockpit window, right at the middle of the boy's chest. He was looking down at the outer layer of the three layer material crinkling up into a hot bubbly mess on him.

'Go go go,' he squealed at the Fly-ahead as he edged his suit zipper down while he slid himself upwards, climbing out of his suit.

Now he was hiding behind the seat in his thin white undersuit, but with one arm still reaching around to hold the accelerator on. The Fly-ahead was going nowhere. The flying suit was smoking and crinkling up smaller and smaller. The purple ray seemed to be getting slightly less bright? The seat was going a different shape as it heated up. There was nothing else to hide behind.

'Why won't you go?' asked the boy of the Fly-ahead, his voice nearly crying.

He suddenly yelled, 'The main power, you idiot!'

He darted out and lunged at a large switch on the centre control panel. The Fly-ahead rocked as the mine launched out of the back. Faint purple light arced across Cort's eyebrow and up his forehead as he squeezed the speed trigger again and was thrown back onto and into the hot seat.

'Ahhhhhh!!' he screamed as the little craft shot madly forward.

He was arching his back away from the seat, and yelling 'the mine the mine the mine', like a warning to himself, and then the camera view went blurry with too many shaky images as the Fly-ahead was thrown forwards through space by a large explosion very near it.

Time had gone by. The camera was on again. Cort was kneeling in front of the seat re-aiming the Fly-ahead, and then resetting a few of the controls. He sounded in a better mood as he chatted to himself.

'Burnt my bum. Third always said if I didn't stop eating them long-life beans my bum would explode one day. My finger didn't bust but. It's only like swoled with a bruise.'

The reflection in the cockpit forward view window showed an ugly blood scabbed scar up Cort's forehead that had split one of his eyebrows, so it had a patch missing in its middle.

'Look, I'll show you again,' he said, taking the camera from his head, 'I've got two hundred hours of everything! That's like a whole planet week. You can rescue me now.'

There was a sad groan from Mr Arthurs, and when Mark looked, he could see wetness in the corner of Mr Arthurs' eye.

'You don't cry, because you're big to look after us,' said Mark quietly.

It was an important unspoken rule, something people should just know.

'I'm sorry Lefty,' Mr Arthurs whispered back, 'Two hundred hours to rescue him is like being given one minute to fit all your school years into, and I've been hoping against everything for a happy ending.'

'It's called "He Died..." ' began Bernard.

'Shh,' interrupted Mr Arthurs, but he wasn't really paying attention to the boys because he was thinking.

'There's plate glue all over the back wall… I know why. It's because…' began James.

'It's called a bulkhead, Dopey, not a wall,' interrupted Bernard.

'Because he's done more of those mine things, to get up speed so he can make it to here, and it's broken him.'

'Broken him!' began Bernard, but his voice fell silent as he thought about the truth of James' words.

Somehow they all just knew, at the same point in time, that James was about to go off. Two little snivelly noises. They all looked across the row to Mr Arthurs.

'Pass him over here,' said Mr Arthurs, like "this is all I need right now".

Yep – James was warming up for a good howl. He knew it too, so he didn't need much shoving towards Mr Arthurs.

'Why does he have to die?' he asked, his voice wobbly sad.

Mark looked across at Shane. Shane had that determined look on his face. He was upset too.

'James! We're like in fourth grade!' said Philip.

He was feeling embarrassed at the theatre full of adults noticing.

'Boys, I don't want to miss the debriefing,' said Mr Arthurs, as he lifted James out of the row, 'Sit quiet. I'm hoping there will be a vote on a rescue attempt. We don't want to miss that do we.'

No, they didn't. They sat still, facing the front, keeping silent, watching the screen. Cort had the helmet off again. He was pointing it at his face, as if he was trying to will a goodbye thought to whoever would watch the film. His skin looked a wrong colour. His eyes were strangely hollow, like emptiness had started growing behind them where there used to be thoughts happening. The fly-ahead boy's shoulder flinched as his cold muscles turned the camera off.

MARK IS FORCED INSIDE THE DECONTAMINATION CHAMBER

'People please remain in their seats. We will empty you row by row into your relevant debriefing rooms. Time is running out, so please pay attention and be ready to move when asked.'

Mark heard James in the distance doing a big sobbing howl. He looked around. He couldn't see Mr Arthurs anywhere in the crowd of adults. A voice came from somewhere behind them.

'I knew it. Look: remember I told you about that Left child attempting to join the community library, to steal books or wreck computers or… whatever, well, there he is – Left child, forcing himself into somewhere inappropriate, again.'

'How can you tell; the whole grubby little pack of them look Left to me.'

'Nah – the one with the haystack hair. See enough of those lost little souls and you just know. I'll sort this. You, Lefty, out from between the seats.'

Mark needed Mr Arthurs. Panic rose in him. He looked to the adults in the rows around, but they were acting like everything was normal.

'Help me?' began Mark, but he swallowed the words as they were leaving him.

Among all these people there was no-one here to help him. Things were getting worse – he heard someone yell, "Stand clear of that child. If there is a problem I will deal with him… I will deal with him". A man in a uniform was coming along the row, moving just as fast as Library man. It was a toss-up which would get Mark first. The trooper was pulling a hand weapon out of its holster, and flicking it to charge.

'Duck,' squeaked Bernard, and they all jumped from their seats to hide down on the floor. Mark waited.

'Move and I will shoot you,' said a voice.

'I'll shoot you,' said Mark back, but of course he didn't have a gun.

'I am just throwing that boy out,' said another voice.

A hand was reaching over the seats.

'You have no authority here. This is a Blue Skies One administered outpost. Do not move,' ordered a voice.

'Cut the heroics, trooper, and don't charge weapons you aren't going to use. I hold an important enough position to get you into some serious trouble, so treat me with respect. That is a Left child, and I do not want it here.'

'I don't want you here,' said Mark, because even though he was afraid, he was also really upset that Library man was ruining a special happening, again.

There was a hum of agreement from the adults standing around waiting to leave their seats, like a sneaky in their throats cheer that he had spoken up for himself.

'People here seem to be forgetting who authorises their government funding,' said Library Man, sounding grim.

A hand was searching, reaching down between the seats to grab a boy. Got Philip by mistake. Dropped him. Mark could see a white pattern in the shape of fingers on Philip's neck. A white pattern made from being held painfully hard. Reaching again. Mark squashed himself right down against the floor, and hid his head beneath the seat in front. He felt the big hand getting a grip on his neck. Pulling at him, and then there was an odd zinging noise, a sharp electrocution jolt went all the way through him, and the hand was gone.

His heart was racing, thumping hard and high in his chest, and he couldn't get enough air. He got slowly to his feet. He was having trouble keeping his balance.

'Woah...' said Bernard like he was thinking, 'Lefty, you've gone weird.'

He didn't need to be told – he could feel it. His clothes were standing out from him like they were allergic to him, and so was his hair. A strange faint tingle began echoing in him, like a memory of when he was in the scout's little stingray craft, before he even came to this planet. For a moment everyone stared at him, and him at them, and then the lights went out. He felt icy, deep fear. It shot straight to the soles of his feet in sharp fizzing zaps of his nerves. He couldn't see anything. Not even dark air right in front of his face. His eyes had stopped working. He heard Bernard panicking.

"I can't see. I can't see".

A voice close in the dark said,

'Get those children out of here. Anywhere for now. My office will do.'

'Yes Sir. Just adjusting our darkfall gear Sir.'

'Then do it faster. Now is not the time to be playing with gadgets.'

'Yes Sir.'

There was an announcement in the dark:

'We have picked up a radiation decay signal from a prohibited weapon. Do not move. Everyone remain silent and stay where you are until we have isolation.'

There was movement close by in the dark, and then talking.

'One each, or two?'

'One – they're squirmy little buggers at that age. Your no-light visor is leaking. Better. There's four of them – you will have to take two, I'll pass them out.'

'Hey, excuse me! I was shot at,' Library man's voice said, and then he went on to mutter, 'and it's wrecked my pocketMusic… and my bloody camera!'

'Shut up or I will shoot you myself, and it will be set to cavity evacuation,' said someone under their breath.

'Trooper, behave yourself.'

'Yes Sir. Sorry Sir.'

Silence in the dark. They were being carried somewhere. Mark heard Philip ask "What does that mean? That cavity thing?".

'Cavity evacuation? Makes you throw up, pee, and poo your pants. Good way of stopping someone from doing things they shouldn't be doing. Quiet now kid until we're clear of the theatre, or I'll give you a turn of it.'

'Will not,' said Philip like a dare.

'Do it?' said Mark, like it would be fun.

Silence, and the tramp of the troopers' feet.

The Base commander's office wasn't very big. It had windows on every wall that looked into rooms all around that were a bit lower. The commander would be like a spider in the middle of its web. The four of them sat where they'd been told, and waited. There were people in those rooms now. From where he was sitting Mark could see the tops of heads. He was just about to stand up for a better look when the door opened. The man didn't come all the way in – he was talking to someone out in the passage.

'The signature was real. We have to retest until we find it. Keep them all moving into the debriefing rooms. As soon as they're in get started, but no-one leaves today until we find where that radiation signature came from.'

'Sir?... It could have been the hand weapon? If it was faulty?'

'No. Thanks for the suggestion, but we are talking some form of class seven weapon radiation residue. That doesn't come from a piddly little stun gun. Someone in that theatre has been hanging around an operational battlecruiser's weapons systems. And it was a battlecruiser from somewhere that isn't part of the Commongood treaty. We need to get to the bottom of this and fast: this is a serious heads up for the survival of this outpost, and the security of this planet. Oh… hello boys. If sitting like that means you are thinking of leaving that chair, don't.'

The man began talking out into the passage again.

'Send that teacher and the other boy to me here. And keep focused on our other objective. Don't forget we are on a tight schedule. Lose a minute and we could lose a life. The vote must go ahead within this hour.'

'Yes Sir. There is an update on timings Sir?'

'Yes?'

'If the Fly-ahead is where we think, we have four hours and forty-three minutes to get an intercepting craft up and positioned.'

'Very well.'

The Base commander turned around as he was closing the door, stood and stared at the boys as if they were animals in a zoo that had got out of their cages, and then he gave them an order.

'Sit still… and… keep quiet… make that silent,' and then he watched them for a moment.

The four of them stared back.

'Well that worked better than I expected.'

'He got shot,' said Shane, breaking the silence and poking Mark with a finger.

Shane said it like the man was supposed to do something about it.

'And he still isn't normal,' added Philip.

Mark crossed his feet over each other, then his eyes, and poked his tongue crooked inside his mouth.

'How can you tell?' asked the man.

Mark knew the man was making fun of them – it was obvious from how his hair was sticking out, making his head into a weird fuzzball, that he wasn't normal again yet. Bernard didn't pick up it was a joke.

'Coz his mouth's not working, Stupid. Not like: yarp yarp yarp, like when he's normal. His sort of normal.'

'Hey! Thanks a lot! Yarp yarp yarp yourself,' said Mark.

'Cured,' said the man, a crooked smile on his face.

'He should have like doctoring,' pointed out Philip.

'Yes,' said Shane, like he didn't think the man was very good because he hadn't made doctoring happen yet.

The man laughed and held his head.

'You are not doing this to me. Not now. We are in the middle of things. I command a whole Outpost. Four small boys in home-made jumpers are not bringing me down. Shhh!... Shhh! Uh?…UH?… better… No – quiet. Shut up! And for Pete's sake stop squirming. Just because your mouths aren't working doesn't mean your legs have to wriggle instead. Thank you. I will do you a deal. Here's the game: your side is – you keep still and quiet. My side is: I will explain to you what's going on. If… shush… if you have to ask a question, wait until I'm ready, and then point.'

'A question – that would be a first,' commented Mr Arthurs, as he came in the door with James.

'Base medic to my office. Full kit. I want the child that got sideblast given a good going over…. Yes, why not.'

It seemed the Base commander could hear a conversation in his ear that no one else could.

'Full decontamination for you,' said the commander, like it was fun for him to have that happen to Mark.

They heard running noises coming their way. Troopers carrying something big. The troopers had trouble getting the thing in through the doorway. They tipped it up on its end. It was a tall motley dirt coloured box. A trooper opened a door in the side.

'It's dirty,' Mark said, already worried that they wanted to shut him inside it.

'No, it's camouflaged.'

'I'm not going in there.'

'Whatever you say.'

'It's too big,' added Mark.

It was a grown man size machine.

'We'll raise the floor platform. Look: just you size.'

'It…' began Mark, looking for more excuses, 'looks dumb.'

'Oh yes, and on a scale of one to ten, how much dumbness is it looking?' asked one of the troopers.

'More even: dumb as you,' offered Mark.

The other trooper laughed.

'Come on kid, don't go weird on me,' said the first trooper, 'I have to do what I'm told, and that means you're going in, whether you like it or not.'

'So like it,' suggested the other trooper with a grim laugh. 'Good fella,' he added, as he grabbed hold of Mark, lifted him and started pushing him in. Mark kicked as good as he could, and aimed carefully so it would count.

'Ooooff,' said the trooper as he crouched over, but he didn't let go of Mark.

'What? Get him in there!'

'Little bastard just kicked me in the nuts!'

The other trooper laughed.

' 'Bout time you took one for the team.'

'Don't do that again kid. Now shut the door, and put your clothes in there. It's not going to hurt: it takes readings of what you breathe in and out, stuff like that. Washes your clothes. Checks out a few other things, and hopefully discharges your hair, because you're looking pretty weird right now brat. And put your clothes back on before you open the door,' added the medic trooper as Mark's feet found the platform inside.

'No,' Mark answered, and kicked at the door while he pushed. He didn't want it to shut all the way.

'Yes,' said the trooper, pushing back from the outside.

'Will the light keep working if the door shuts?'

'Good one,' said the trooper medic like Mark was being funny, and shoved harder until the door clicked closed.

There was hissing around the door. Seals fattening up. The light inside wasn't very bright. The air smelt funny. He could still hear voices outside.

'No clothes in the decontamination rinse.'

'Little bugger. They're all ears and eyes, but they don't listen to a word you say.'

'Could be payback – not doing what he's told, because we won the big battle of the door shutting.'

'Then we're even, little bugger. It's not funny – it friggin hurt. He's got nasty pointy little feet, and you should have seen the look on his face: he bloody well meant it.'

'One all then,' and then the first trooper laughed.

It was a silly, "I've got an idea" laugh.

'Breathing tube his mouth and we'll wash the lot.'

'Do a germ count while we're at it.'

Adult chuckles from outside. Mark knew he was being made fun of.

'Germ count yourself you big crap head,' he yelled.

The door was suddenly open again, and a trooper was grabbing at him.

'I'm doing it I'm doing it,' said Mark pulling a shoe off, but the trooper had his head in an arm lock, and was shoving something onto his face that suckered onto the skin around his mouth nose and eyes. It wouldn't come off.

'You won't get it off. And, hey, keep it nice, okay kid? We were just having a bit of fun. No need to turn nasty on us.'

The door shut. He thought the thing he was in was filling with warm bubbly water. Fear rose in him, as the "water" got to his nose, then his eye level, and still kept going up. He stood on tip toes, trying to keep his face clear. The watery stuff was above his eyebrows the next time he tried to breathe, because he had to. His lungs sucked desperately, breathing something in, and then he could see there was only a tiny bit of water, floating on top of some sort of gas. Suddenly something was squirting him up the nose, and all through his mouth. Now he couldn't breath. There were bubbles on his eyes. He panicked, kicking and hitting the inside walls of the decontamination chamber for help.

'Calm down calm down. It's all right kid – it's only for a moment. See, better now?'

Warm air began making his clothes billow out from him like sails. There was a readout happening in lights on the wall in front of his face.

"Recently acquired germs, body mass index comparison: 24% (low). Resident surface germ population, body mass adjusted figure… You had twelve times more resident germs than an average creature your size."

He heard laughing outside. He couldn't say anything back because his mouth was blocked with the breather tube.

"Industrial chemical contaminants… clean. Military contaminants… clean. Radiation residues…"

A nasty fat dull beeping began, and the light inside the decontamination chamber turned to flashing acid red. He heard someone yell,

'Get him out, get him out.'

JAMES MAKES THINGS HAPPEN

Mark was standing in the middle of the room feeling his hair slowly coming back down to normal. He had never been so clean in his whole life. He was so clean he felt like a layer of something he normally wore was missing.

'My germs protect me,' he muttered to himself.

He sent a finger up inside his nose. There was nothing there at all.

'I haven't even got any snot,' he said, feeling like he'd been invaded.

Nobody was listening. The troopers had gone back to wherever they came from. The Base commander and Mr Arthurs were over at a large screen looking things up. They had become very paly.

'Here was I thinking the planet was about to be attacked, and it's just one child with a radiation inspired cell memory triggered by some sideblast.'

'Don't you worry, he's destructive enough. Having fun doesn't usually involve tidiness and peace and quiet. There, what is that line referring to? Acquired radiation signature... No?'

'Cellular overlay... no, not that either. I don't think we're going to find our answer. The marker is there in him... all through him. It will be from some prohibited weapon, and outposts like this don't have access to that sort of information. You have to wonder where a small boy would come across that sort of thing?'

'Space orphan.'

'Even so... and how did he manage to survive it? I can't log this as a question; it would be like tagging him to be experimented on. Best keep this to ourselves: no names, no record, no inquiries. How are you feeling now boy?'

'I think my head's getting swollen?'

'Lefty, behave. That's his joke, because I say it every time he gets attention for the pictures he draws. He's a good drawer, our Lefty. We could try "residual markers in biological material"?'

Shane Philip and Bernard were sitting impatiently on their chairs, watching James. Bernard looked like it was killing him not to be doing what James was doing. James was cruising along the front of the huge control console that went nearly all the way around the room, his hand reaching up and over to brush across all the control buttons, seeing what it felt like to be the person who would push them.

'He's going to press something, like "it was an accident!" and then we all get in trouble,' said Shane, not like he was bothered, but more like "here we go again".

'You can bet on that,' said Bernard, 'If it's not Lefty smart-arse joking us into detention it's Sook Boy doing what he does.'

'Am not going to,' said James, annoyed.

'Are too,' said Mark, happy with the thought of some action.

James looked back at him.

'You can say that because you're not being mean,' he stated.

He came to a large green button, big enough for a whole little hand to go over.

'I'm not pushing it,' he said, like he meant "get off my case", 'but I bet it does something interesting,' he added, his hand covering it as he felt the texture on its surface.

'No! No, that's the "initiate my changes" button!'

The Base commander had James by one arm, holding him away from the console.

'What have you done?'

'I didn't touch anything!'

'Did too,' said Bernard from his seat, 'you like touched the whole lot of everything.'

'I mean I didn't push anything. Not one thing.'

'There are no push buttons in here,' said the Base commander angrily, 'Your little pink mitts block the light to a switch, and then things happen. So let's see what you've happened to us today, shall we?'

Through the viewing windows all the rooms being looked into had gone misty, like they were inside clouds.

'For a start you are dampwash air freshening our guests with carpet cleaner.'

The commander's hands were racing all over the big console, covering switch after switch, readjusting everything as fast as he could.

'Get a trooper in here now. I want all of console three reset… and four. How many? How many buttons did you press child?'

James was too shocked to speak. He stared up at the huge man and tried not to cry.

'All of them,' said Mr Arthurs quietly, 'That's how they learn. As far as he could reach.'

He picked James up and put him on a seat.

'Stay there quietly for a while, while we sort this out,' was all he said.

The commander was still hovering over the consoles while a trooper worked correcting things.

'Cleaner robots roaming free, no thankyou… that was hallway lighting and temperatures… that is not an appropriate wallscreen saver for the juniortroopers' dorm… and what is this?' The commander laughed like he was caught by surprise.

'First you set the floor polishers on the loose, and now you've turned all the troopers' lockers out onto the decks for a surprise inspection. Parade uniforms holiday clothes underwear socks and all. You will be unpopular.'

RUNNING OUT OF TIME FOR SOMETHING IMPORTANT

A trooper appeared at the door out to the passage.

'Sir, there's some sort of crisis in the accommodation – clothes everywhere.'

'Really?' said the commander, like he was mildly interested.

'It's really bad Sir. All our lockers are empty, and it's like the cleaning robots are having a swimming competition in all our gear. Duty valet thinks it might be a glitch in the autofunctions.'

'Yes seniortrooper, I wouldn't be surprised, but you can tell the duty valet the glitch season is over: all five glitches are here with me. Have the mess sorted and cleared away.'

'Of course Sir. I would have already Sir, but we're running out of time? Debriefing rooms are seated and sealed?'

'Thank you. I am aware. Commence the program. SIC will be OIC: I am dealing with a situation.'

'Yes Sir.'

'What's SIC?' asked Philip, and they all giggled.

'Second In Command,' said the commander, 'and OIC is Officer In Charge, and, before you ask me, the "situation" is you. The five of you.'

'Well we had a deal,' said Bernard, a bit stroppy.

'Yes…,' said the commander.

He was thinking.

'Boys, I need your teacher's voice out there, because things are dangerously close to disaster for our little friend in the Fly-ahead, so John is going to debriefing room one now, to try to sway the arguments. I need to be here to keep an eye on everything, so you can stay here with me? Shall we begin our deal now? Good.'

'But you have to tell us stuff,' said Shane, determined.

A hand held up – the Base commander was listening to a voice in his ear.

'Right. You boys are my advisory panel. We are hunting for a happy ending for Cort. We don't know for certain that he has died. Here is the situation: Outer 17 voted yesterday to refuse us permission to use their rescue craft. I believe that was because if the Fly-ahead crashes onto the planet they will have salvage rights to any rare materials or technologies. On the other hand, if we were to rescue the little craft as it reaches the outer atmosphere, and the pilot was to live, then he and his machine would remain Star Triangle property, and we must do our best to return them. That would leave Outer 17 with nothing but the rescue bill. We agreed to have a recount on their decision after we had shown the film. That is where we are up to now; a fresh vote on whether to attempt a rescue. What now?'

Five arms were up in the air, like 'teacher, teacher'.

'We're voting,' explained Shane.

'I… um… see this heads up display on the window… wait while I get it there… now, I'm sorry, but do you see your names?'

'Yep, there's Planetti, and Shane, and me.'

'I see... Even Base commanders can get good breaks. Wastelands Area Community reps. I think your teacher has pulled a swifty. Wait while I log you in… Five votes for crash and salvage rights?'

The commander looked surprised by the squeaky howls of anger. 'Hey! Joking! I was joking. I thought you'd laugh. It was a good joke?'

'No.'

'Boy, you lot are tough work. So, five votes for…'

'Don't,' said Shane, 'this is very serious.'

'Hmmm. Wait… All the votes are in out there. Not good. Now I'm adding yours. This is too close for comfort. Something else is going on. Final tally,' said the commander, running his fingers over the console to change the display.

'Um, kids, this is where you need some explaining to: even though we might win the vote, they will have other tricks up their sleeves to get the outcome they want. They are politicians, and that's what they do: work hard to get the result they think is right. We don't agree with them this time, but… So… there you go; just over the line; we can have a rescue attempt. Worth a cheer but now let's see how play goes from here.'

'That was a lot of words,' said James.

'Yes. Well let me try again: the whole thing in less words… They forced a vote, with only big business and a military commander or two getting a say, I didn't like the outcome, so I made them show the film to a wider representation of this planet's people, they sweet-talked and threatened everyone to reach an outcome that had them win by four votes, but, but, hang on there, you are a toey little bunch aren't you, then I added in your votes.'

'That's not really true,' said Philip.

'You're just sucking up,' added Bernard, 'so we think we had a go of being needed.'

'I'm afraid it is true. They calculated how many votes, called in that many favours, made that many threats, and didn't even notice you. Your five votes caught them by surprise.'

'You're a bit hopeless,' said Mark, 'coz that's still too many words.'

'And you could do better, my friend who complains about being short on snot?'

'Yep: they cheated, you caught them out, they cheated some more.'

'Is that it?'

'Yep, and now you're going to fix it.'

'Yes. Perhaps. All right, I give up. Let me find out what's happening.'

The commander was listening to his ear again. Holding his hand up in case the boys should speak.

'Now the truth is coming closer. Of course they want that boy to survive as much as you do, but they are hiding something. I think this is the real reason they don't want a rescue to happen: they know it can't be successful, because the money we gave them to fuel-core their rescue craft has vanished into their pockets instead, and the craft is useless, stuck on the ground, so they are stalling until it is too late to do anything, in the hope that they won't be found out. Well, there go all our chances.'

The Base commander's voice had gone grey, hard and sad.

' 'nother plane?' suggested James hopefully.

'Not a plane, a high altitude manoeuvrable recovery rocket. This is a small half empty planet at the far outreaches of nowhere. They had only the one, sorry lad. Next time. Another year, another rescue, we'll do better.'

'No. No,' said James, already half in tears.

'Shush Jimbo, it's not over,' said Bernard, 'we know a plane, and it goes real high, like until the sky isn't even blue any more.'

'I'm getting advice on that, right now,' said the commander, with one hand on his ear.

'Add two crew… the weight is? Too much. Boys, that plane; you mean the Happy Flier? You must, because it's the only high altitude craft on this planet. Well, it is a powered glider, it already weighs slightly more than can get to the altitude we need, the altitude at which the atmosphere will begin burning a speeding Fly-ahead, especially a damaged one, and being a glider it is so lightly built we can't attach rescue gear to it. Then we'd need two crew – a pilot and a rescue tether operator. That poor flimsy glider would have trouble just getting itself up there.'

'It got us and all our mums up there,' pointed out Philip.

'And they're pretty fat,' added Bernard.

'They'd weigh more than a rescue thing?' suggested Shane.

'There is "up there", and then there is up there high enough, and in exactly the right place. We are trying our hardest,' was the commander's reply.

'Don't you boys go thinking we aren't. It is a secret outside this room, but planet Terra have dispatched a high speed emergency hospital ship at my request. It won't get here until some time tonight, but to send a ship half way across a galaxy at top speed is a big commitment. A very big commitment.'

What was the point of a hospital ship, if the patient had already crashed and died by then? They sat in a row on their chairs, silent, aware of the sadness of failure. Of being needed by someone, another boy like them, desperately needed, and they had failed to make happiness happen for him.

'It can't land anyway,' commented Mark, 'Miss Shandy says high speed full size ships can never land on planets, because it's too hard to get them off again.'

OUR PLAN IS THE BEST

'I'm not sitting on a chair any more. They're the wrong size,' said Philip, and he sat with a thump on the floor.

'Me neither,' said Shane, like it was a pay-back against grown-ups for not rescuing the Fly-ahead boy.

The commander was back at his console listening to his ear. They all sat in a circle on the floor.

'We could have done it. If we were them we could,' said Shane.

'Yeah,' said Bernard, 'we would have put the fuel core in, and then the rescue rocket thing would fly when we needed it.'

'No, I mean we would make things work now. We would take bits off the Happy Flier until it was light enough, like we do at Space Cadets, when we unbolt the seats and stuff for a change around. We would think of things.'

'Yeah, and Lefty could pilot, because he did already, that plane he did, and I could fire the tether and work the communicator… Well, maybe it doesn't have to be exactly me,' said Bernard.

They all looked at James. He was the smallest, the lightest.

'You're the best one anyway Sook Guts,' went on Bernard, 'coz you do what you're told. Sometimes I'm not good at that,' he added as an afterthought.

'It's a plan?' asked James, a brittle shaft of happiness in his voice.

'Lefty?'

Mark was supposed to know. To make a decision.

'The emergency tether is only for firing at a rescue rocket, for like if the Happy Flier gets in trouble, so it can get towed back,' said Mark.

There was a sadness in knowing things. Things about flying out into space. Knowledge shrank the possibilities. They all felt the commander above them.

'It was only a game,' said Philip defensively, 'we were only playing. We're allowed.'

'I happen to like your game. A bit of knowledge and the possibilities begin to grow don't they: a self targeting tow tether is just what we need, if it is fired at the right time, then the Fly-ahead will tow you as you slow it down, and do you know why they have fly-ahead boys? Because they take up less space and weigh so much less than adult crew. So – not such a silly plan. How about you all go outside and have a look at the Happy Flier through the fence, while us grown ups see what other plans we can come up with?'

'He's the flier, the pilot man, for our plan,' said Bernard pointing at Mark, 'Our plan is the best,' he added.

'Then you two had better go out and have a practice then, you Lefty, and... Sook Guts, was it?'

'No,' objected James, shy awkward, and laughing at the insult to himself at the same time.

'Okay, I know it isn't. Your friend here might call me Stupid, but stupids aren't usually left in command of space outposts. Off you go now James my hero, and his gang.'

They were half way down the passage when Mark thought of something.

'I'm going to go back and ask if we can tell Mr Kopter to get the Happy Flier ready,' he said.

He got to the door. He could hear the Base Commander talking to his ear again.

'I sent them next door to annoy Avro. Told them to just look through the fence, but we know how long that will last.'

He stood there listening, his heart saddened. Why didn't grown ups allow them to do anything that mattered?

'I don't like this plan to use slingshot rocket capture nets to bring it down. How can that lessen the impact? They are just after having it land where they can get to the wreckage first... You would have been proud of your boys. Their plan was good... a ridiculous idea though when you consider their age... Yes, we'd end up with two dead children and a wrecked plane, in exchange for an attempted rescue of an alien boy who is probably already dead, or so close to it it doesn't matter... So this is another 'negotiated compromise' ending. Really poor. Every time I am forced into this, I tell myself this is not to happen again, and then next time it's the same old story; no money, or not enough resources, or someone else is more entitled, or there is some obscure law in the way... I think we are nearly done here. I can't contact the hospital ship to ask them to turn back – they are on silent running so they can come and go undetected... No, nothing sneaky; just so Outer 17 didn't feel imposed upon, so people wouldn't feel I was making decisions for them before they had a chance to decide for themselves. In the end this is not my planet.'

Words words words, with nothing good happening. Mark walked slowly away, back down the passage to the others.

'Let's go see the plane,' was all he said.

'Lollies?' asked James.

'Yes,' he said, but not happy, more like he no longer cared.

Once again, like that library day, lollies came too late. Unhappiness had got to him first.

THE RESCUE BEGINS

'Well hello there,' Avro said in greeting, as he placed a spanner down.

Five small boys staring up at him.

'What are you doing?' asked Shane.

'Unbolting a few seats, in case they need my plane for something. Getting her lighter.'

'We came to help.'

'Good. I could do with some help. Mind you – they haven't actually asked me yet, for the Happy Flier I mean.'

'They aren't going to,' said Mark, 'They gave up already.'

'Why?!' asked Avro, like he too wanted to cry, like his feelings were hurt a lot.

'They say she's too heavy, with a full size men crew she is, and they aren't going to let us.'

Avro put the spanner down again. Picked it up, bouncing it on his open palm while he thought.

'So what's their alternative?'

'They are giving up. Saying they've reached a negotiated compromise.'

'Big words for letting us down, hey?'

'Yes,' said Shane.

They were all looking up at Avro still.

'We could do it,' said Philip, his voice more asking than saying.

'We could?' pleaded James.

'And I could ask, but they like saying "no" too much,' said Avro.

'All right... Into the office – let's do the maths again first. I feel like that boy in space is me, me in another turn of life. My heart will break if he dies because we didn't try.'

The maths didn't work out. Avro had all the facts: upper atmosphere jetstream wind speeds, target area microclimate temperature and humidity predictions, even trajectory traces and timings in hundredths of seconds, but two crew were too heavy. Even one man and one boy were too heavy for the Happy Flier to get that high. The big bowl of lollies sat untouched on the little office's coffee table.

'Really close,' said Avro.

'Take more seats out?' suggested James.

'When you discover a way to take out twenty seats, when she only had eighteen in the first place, you let me know.'
Avro looked across at Shane.

'Throw me one, Grubby,' said Avro, 'A sherbety one. I have a plan B, and I like it.'
The mood changed. Armed with lollies they followed him to the back of the hangar, where something sat hidden under a tarp.
'Never showed you this before, did I,' he said, like it was a surprise he'd been saving.
'This is an old fighter left after the LifeWorlds pulled out of the military base. I've been remaking it out of... oh... about seven old wrecks. This year was going to be like the big surprise flight, but I was a bit slow with the last few tests. She, it, he... haven't named it yet, is pretty good, don't you reckon? I like the colours.'

'It still looks a bit broken?' asked Bernard.

'It's got like dents and stuff, and half the paint's missing,' said Philip.

'Yes, but listen to this,' said Avro, leaning into the cockpit to start something.

'Proton sucking backblower. It is the coolest engine.'

'Well I don't hear very much things happening,' said Shane, looking suspicious of Avro and the machine.

'Can't you hear that faint sweet whistle, like a really happy kid stuck on one note?'

Now Avro mentioned it they all could.

'I like the dull silver, and the blue stripe. I even like the dints and scratches,' Avro said proudly.

'It looks like a car people like crashing, with wings stuck on by mistake,' said James, as he stroked the dinted fuselage with exploring fingers.

'We have to hurry,' said Mark.

'Well this is my plan: I follow you up and talk you through everything. It's not like you will be up there on your own. I will be up there too, keeping an eye on you, just a few thousand feet below. It does sound a bit iffy, but that's the only way we can get the Happy Flier up that high, and any lower, and the little Fly-ahead, with nothing to slow it down, will get too hot for anyone to stay alive inside, and the boy pilot will die. Okay, help me get these seats out. We need to unscrew half the controls too and relocate them, and put a seat in front for James.'

READY, SET...

From out in the middle of the airfield the world looked like it was all sky. They hadn't left the ground yet.

'I'm scared,' said James, from where he was strapped into the very front seat.

The long tow rope snaking out from the nose lifted up from the ground. There was a groan. The Happy Flier began to move. Very slowly. There were a few bumping jarring thumps, and a wobbly feeling. Then a groan again as it slowed to a stop. It tilted a little off balance on the old runway surface, and stayed there, large and empty, not going anywhere.

'Maybe he's getting more power going in his motor,' suggested James.

'I wish ours was going,' commented Mark as he ran his fingers over the controls.

He didn't like the idea of starting it somewhere way up in the sky – what if it didn't?

'Lefty?'

James, worrying about something.

'You have to keep it low. He said you have to keep the Happy Flier low until he's off the ground too, or we'll lift his tail up and he'll crash.'

'Hey – I know already, okay?'

'Sorry. I'm scared.'

'Me too, okay?'

Mark looked at the head in front of him. James was like an outside echo of the little kid chicken bit Mark had inside himself. If you told him you felt the same, then he felt better, like he could rely on you to care and understand. Mark didn't actually feel scared yet, more excited, and worried that they wouldn't get up there in time.

The little communicator speaker frightened them both with a sudden blurt noise.

'Okay boys – how are you doing?'

'Good, Mr Kopter,' said James, 'The Happy Flier is really big when you're not here.'

'Thanks. You've got your flight notes? Once we're up I'm going to tow you around in big lazy circles while we gain height. Watch your readouts James, and when… what are you going to do?'

'When we get to each highness, I am going to tell Mark to… start the engine, to… put the wing extensions out, to fly back towards the sun, and to listen to the communicator and turn around when you say.'

'And then it will be ready, set, go as fast as you can. If we are doing everything right, the Fly-ahead will cast a finger shadow below you, but not on you, because the late afternoon sun will be behind it and you, and he will be lower, because he is coming into our atmosphere on a tangent. The air is sort of fuzzy up there: the shadow will be in it, not on it. I've got everything as accurate as I can. You have to make sure you are flying in line with the shadow, or the Happy Flier will be really hard to control when the emergency towline takes up tension. Oh dear… I don't know how many words are too many for you.'

'Tell him that's enough, James. I got all of them,' said Mark.

'Mr Kopter? That's enough times of those words. Mark knows them now, coz you told us everything before already.'

'Thanks James. Sorry, but here's some more: if the Fly-ahead shadow falls on the Happy Flier, the Fly-ahead is above you, and going to hit you. If that happens, you <u>have</u> to dive and swerve to one side, or you will kill him when he rams into you, and all three of you will be a tumbling wrecked ball of flames. If you have to let him go past like that, I will try to catch him when he gets down to my altitude… Hello?'

'We're thinking.'

'Don't. You have to do what you are told up there, or bad things will happen. Sorry.'

'Mark says "we're good".'

'All right. Don't forget I've written down what your gauges should say at each change in what you're doing, and your holding position to wait for him, so you can check for yourselves everything is going right.'

'It's harder to fly without the engine,' said Mark quietly.

'Mark says it's harder to…'

'Shh James! That was just for us.'

'Yes, okay, but after I've towed you up you will still be full of fuel, so if a miracle does happen and we catch the Fly-ahead, and then it tows you away across the wastelands and out over the desert, you will be able to fly back… …You need to let me know when you've heard me.'

'Yes Sir.'

' "Got that" will do, Sook Guts.'

James giggled.

'He called me Sook Guts,' he said.

'Now you remember how to activate the emergency tow? I'll be flying down below, watching you on my battlescreen. We probably won't be able to see each other – we're both too small. I mean I don't know how high I can get in this.'

'Got that.'

Silence. Mark looked down through the cockpit floor window. Cracked concrete of the runway, with tiny bits of dry dead grass in it. He looked out the side cockpit window, over to the Base, where inside, all the "important" grown ups were probably arguing about who should get what, after the fly-ahead smashed into the planet, and the fly-ahead boy was dead. James turned around.

'He's not saying much,' he whispered.

It was then Mark just knew Avro Kopter was chickening out. It was strange, but once he'd thought it, everything felt like that, even the sunlight falling across the information readouts in the cockpit. Even the back of James' head, with its little rooster tail of hair sticking up. Through their communicator they heard Avro clicking switches in his cockpit, while he muttered to himself.

'Neither of them is Alito. Though of course they can't understand that…'

Avro Kopter began to talk to them through the communicator again.

'Boys… I… I've forgotten something. I have to go back to the office. Only for a minute. Sorry. I'll be right back, straight away, I promise. This was a good practise run.'

They watched as Avro climbed down from his plane. He wasn't hurrying. He was walking slowly like he was putting something off, or thinking a lot. He changed his mind half way back to the hangar, and turned towards the base building. Walking, walking, way over there. The tiny figure in the distance went inside. The entrance doors shut, the sunlight glinting off them as they did it.

'He's gone to ask them, hasn't he. I know coz it's like me dobbing. They won't let us, will they.'

'No.'

'My mum would let me? Coz it's a good thing, isn't it. To rescue someone is a good thing.'

Deep inside Mark a large emptiness was growing, a feeling like he was really old. He was looking at James' face, wide trusting eyes looking up and back at him, and then Mark understood, clearer than he'd understood anything ever before. There was no way, ever, that James' mum would let James be here, doing this, risking everything he was. Mark could almost hear her crying now, as she held onto a small dead crumpled body.

'Hey? Go tell the others I'm... we're going anyway, while I get the tow unhooked? We have to be quick, before Avro comes back.'

'Got that, Captain,' said James, 'I'll tell them they have to stay behind,' and then he was working the door mechanism, tipping out the boarding ladder, and scrambling down from the plane.

GO

The pull release knob inside had worked, but the towline hook hadn't dropped out. He climbed down to look. It was leaning up against the glider. For something that was supposed to be lightweight it was hard for a ten-year-old to move. It fell with a whack down onto the concrete. He looked around as he was climbing back up into the Happy Flier. James must still be in the hangar. He pulled the ladder in. Swung the door shut. The door seal had to be inspected. Yes. Now, quick, strap himself into the harness, and... um... was that everything? Hurry, hurry. No, that must be everything before starting the engine, because they had been ready to go before. Hand on the engine ignition lever, waiting to pull it across. Now... or never. Like the escape pod of his broken Family ship, with only his sisters in it and him still outside, he had to make this big decision. He remembered the fly-ahead boy's face, the eyes, silently screaming 'help me'. No-one was going to help if he didn't. Nobody, ever, and soon it would be too late. I am doing it, because he is just a boy like me, and I don't want to feel rotten about this for the rest of my life, decided Mark. The switch clunked across from the pressure of his fingers. The engine hummed quietly as it warmed into life. Wheel brakes off. Steering the front wheel so the Happy Flier would go around the tow cable, and around the fighter plane still sitting in the middle of the runway. Leaving the concrete of the runway. Bumping across the uneven little tufts of dry grass that were the rest of the airfield. Turning sharply back in front of the fighter to get back onto the runway centre line, in case there wasn't going to be enough runway left. Wheel brakes on. Wing brakes out. Engine up. He glanced quickly towards the hangar. No James yet, running towards the plane crying, hurt he was being left behind. Now. Mark had to go now, before that happened.

The Happy Flier began to roll, the uneven runway surface vibrating the whole plane as the wheels turned.

He focused his eyes on the runway ahead, and told his thoughts to leave everything behind on the ground, everything except flying the plane and rescuing the fly-ahead boy.

The old runway was huge. Faster and faster along it the Happy Flier went. He was panicking that the end was somewhere just ahead when the wheels went quiet, no longer running over the broken concrete and dead grass. He was in the air. Very wobbly, and feeling like it would be easy for a wing to dip and cause a bad crash landing, but he was off the ground. He pulled in the wing brakes, and the Happy Flier began rising so fast he was nearly sick. He must have come really close to it, because now he could smell it, sick, in the air of the cockpit. Up, up, rising so much faster than the cadet club flight. He suddenly realised: there was no weight left in the plane, no cadet club, no mums, no Miss Shandy, no grown man pilot, no seats, no lunch boxes, no drinks for everyone, hardly anything to lift at all, so of course it would go up into the sky faster. The altitude meter's numbers where changing so quickly they were a blur. Only the number on the left was still, and now it had just become a three... a four... a five. An alarm was sounding, a little panicking chirp: he was rising into the sky too fast for the plane's systems to get everything ready for high altitude flying. There was a squirt of warm air from somewhere: the cabin heater had kicked in. He levelled the Happy Flier out, and began to rise slower, in big lazy circles.

Even the Spaceport tower was small down below him now. Everything seemed under control. What was supposed to happen next? While he was looking down out of the cockpit window there was a paper crumpling noise. James' reminder sheet, stuck on under James' controls for the communicator and the emergency tow release. It must have shifted, started to fall off in the air from the heater. He was glad it had made a noise, because it was just what he needed now. It was a bit far away to read clearly... what was that number, the one next to 'altitude'? Woah, he was already higher than when he should have put the wing extensions out. Where was that? Was it a switch, or a lever? Lever. He knew it was a lever, from before. How could he forget? He was panickier than he thought, so he wasn't thinking all the things he should.

'Calm down, and concentrate,' he told himself.

Today was not allowed to end with two dead boys. Two boys both a long way from home. He wondered what the Star Triangle worlds were like. The wing extension parts made a fizzy whirring sound, followed by a click as they locked into place. Now... what was next? Position. He had to get to an exact position in the sky. He peered over his controls at James' sheet. He was two kilometres too low, still, and way off course: right over on the far side of the sky was where he should be. Banking into a turn... beginning to sideslip. Don't turn so hard. The Happy Flier was even harder to fly when she was this light, almost as if the air could carry her where-ever it liked, because even though she was big, with long thin wings spanning out into the sky, she had no weight. He was surprised she felt this clumsy though, like she still had air brakes on. He checked them again. It was like Avro had said, things had to be done slowly, with slight, gentle adjustments.

HIGH IN THE SKY, TOO HARD FOR JUST ONE BOY BY HIMSELF

He was higher even than cadet club Space Day. A lot. He could see the curve of the planet from up here. The temperature readout for outside had jammed at minus sixty. The air here wasn't even. It was almost in lumps, making the Happy Flier wallow around, rising and falling, slipping sideways, and trembling while she did it. The airframe was groaning and creaking. Lots of little orange lights were blinking lazily on the controls. If any began to blink

faster he would have to lose altitude right away, because it meant
something was breaking, some part of the plane wasn't surviving
the lack of pressure outside, or the extreme coldness. He thought
he was where he should be. The time was right. Something
should happen, some time real soon. A lot of sky. A lot of 'what
ifs' too, like what if the Deep Space listening station had got the
calculations wrong for the course the Fly-ahead was on, or the
time it would take to get here? What if it did come when and
where it was supposed to, but it was bouncing on the atmosphere
too, and bounced into the Happy Flier? Worse than anything else,
a new fear soaked through him: was this already over? He was
remembering those sounds in the middle of the night, the high
speed tearing of the sky, and the distant thump of something
smashing into the planet. It could have been the end of the fly-
ahead boy, and his little spacecraft. At this totally wrong moment
a laugh came out of him. He had surprised himself with a cartoon
memory; Planetman saying "not now, I'm concentrating on
getting a happy ending". It was when Planetman was upside
down smashing through buildings with bits falling off his space
ship, and then he just reached around next to his seat and said,
"there it is! Found my lunch", as if that fixed everything. The
moral was believe things will work out, and get on with what you
were doing. Yes, but what am I doing, he thought. If the Fly-
ahead was coming, then soon the Happy Flier would be a flaming
ball of tumbling wreckage, shattered by the Fly-ahead as they
both fell from the sky, or he would still be flying, but watching
the Fly-ahead speed by, unrescued. He knew this because he had
a real big problem: he couldn't reach the emergency tow release
from his pilot seat, and he couldn't let go of the controls for even
the tiniest fraction of time to get to it, because he was only just
staying in control now, by being extra careful to keep his hands
still and steady. Losing control for even one tiny moment would
leave the Happy Flier yawing and sideslipping uncontrollably out
of the sky, down, down down, and the Fly-ahead would race
overhead to its doom. He sat there thinking. Twenty-three
seconds to go. This was why there were supposed to be two boys
in this cockpit. He tried to reach underneath his control panel
with his foot, but the back of the seat put in for James was in the
way. He loosened his harness, and really carefully moved his

bum across on his pilot seat. He stretched his leg out again. Fifteen seconds to go. Still something was in the way. He couldn't figure out what, because it felt a bit soft, and there was nothing soft left in the plane. He shoved at it again, but although it was soft, it wouldn't move. He saw a shadow getting darker in a long finger shape beneath the Happy Flier. The Fly-ahead was coming. The Fly-ahead was coming! Everything was going to happen just like Mr Kopter said: dead boys in flaming wrecks. The Happy Flier wobbled dangerously as he struggled to get out of his harness fast enough to get to the tow release in time. It had to be fired any second now. He was out of the harness, but he had to fall back into his seat and grab at the controls again, because he'd just lost enough height to sink into the shadow, meaning a massive crash was about to happen. He felt unprotected without the harness on, dangerously loose. The Happy Flier rose sluggishly. The shadow was getting darker. He looked at the emergency tow-release firing button like he wanted to will it to work with his eyes. There was a little pink finger over it. A little pink finger... Then he noticed a thin stick of hair sticking up over the front edge of his control panel.

'Now?' asked a familiar voice, 'is it now?'

'No. No,' said Mark, as he panicked getting his safety harness back on, 'get in your seat properly. Get your harness on.'

'You didn't put our wheels up yet,' squeaked James back, his voice urgent.

In the middle of everything else Mark managed to find the wheels controller. He could hear them winding up into the fuselage at the same time as his safety harness clicked together. The Happy Flier softly surged forward, moving slightly faster, and then even faster, accelerating through the thin air.

He waited. Now he was afraid. The Happy Flier was a big floating around in the sky flimsy target. The Fly-ahead, crashing down through the atmosphere, was a space-strong wedge shaped piece of plummeting metal. Soon something would happen, and it could be really bad. James's voice suddenly squeaked quickly, higher even than usual –

'You're my best friend?'

'We're not dying yet,' said Mark.

His eyes were straining, looking at that shadow finger in the misty-cloudiness. It seemed to be getting clearer, and clearer. When should the towline be launched? Too early and there would be nothing to catch. Too late and the Fly-ahead would shoot past, become a burning ball, and smack into the planet.

'Wait...wait,' he said.

A whooshing noise buffeted the Happy Flier. Mark had a horrible feeling, that was screaming "too late" inside his head – the Fly-ahead boy had just passed, dangerously close, and going very fast. In his panic Mark couldn't get his voice working.

'NOW,' he screamed finally.

There was a loud 'crack' like the Happy Flier was breaking apart, and a black line was snaking out into the sky ahead, the other end of it spraying out rocket flame in towhead positioning fingers.

'Wing extensions in, motor full speed,' James read out quickly, so quickly it was more gibbering than words.

'Doing it doing it.'

'You were s'posed to be going fast as anything already... and you didn't have to kick me: I was already awake. I was trying to decide if the the tow thing should be "front" or "back". Mr Kopter forgot there is a deciding, because he never said "two switches James, and it's that one".'

'Hands in the air,' yelped Mark in a panic.

He wanted those touchy-feely fingers where he could see them, not hovering over switches they didn't understand.

'The one with "front" on it felt better anyway,' said James, 'so it's too late?'

'Yeah. Put your hands down then,' said Mark.

The towline reel was still spinning, and line was whizzing from the front of the Happy Flier, out across the sky. She was flying better now, with the wheels where they should be, instead of out like huge air brakes. She was roaring across the sky, but was this fast enough? James was right – the Happy Flier was supposed to be at full speed before the tow line tried to reach the crashing Fly-ahead. If it wasn't fast enough, the towline wouldn't be able to catch up with the Fly-ahead, and then it wouldn't lock onto it, and then... everything would turn out bad. After starting out so good. They flew out of the mistiness, into clear sky. There was a little shape way ahead. His eyes were on the emergency towline. It was sort of stretching across the sky in that direction, in wiggly coils. Suddenly it turned into a huge wobbly arc, that was straightening out, and spinning the little thing on the far end around.

'It's got it by the front!' squealed James.

The line began wobbling like a huge guitar string, the wobbles getting quicker and quicker.

'Uh-oh,' said James, 'here we go.'

Mark realised his teeth were clenched, and his knuckles, where his hands were hanging onto the Happy Flier's controls, were white from holding on so hard.

The line tightened with a humming zing, and the Happy Flier wrenched forwards, making Mark's head hit the seat headrest so hard his eyes couldn't focus any more. He tried to keep the controls steady, but everything was blurred, and racing faster and faster into his eyes.

'We're going upside down!' he heard James squeak.

'All right. I can't see properly. I'll fix it.'

Now he knew the world was the coloured blur above his head he could work at righting the Happy Flier, and getting that yellow coloured blur back under his feet. His arms were straining at the controls when something wet splattered in his face, and began running through his hair.

'I thought I sicked up everything before!' said James.

A lump of something slid down his neck. His nose couldn't hide from the smell. He felt his Mothers' Day lollies rising through his throat. He couldn't stop them. He had to keep control of the plane. He mustn't get it on all the readouts and switches. He leant forward, tried to get it to go beyond them. In the middle of everything, the fear and the panic, he couldn't help giggling at the next thing James said.

'Hey! That's disgusting! You sicked! All over me!'

His eyes were nearly normal again. The Happy Flier was the right way up. She was going so fast now that pressure cushion clouds were formed around the nose, and on the front edges of the wings, like hazy white pillows. Mark couldn't see the Fly-ahead any more, if it was the Fly-ahead out there. The emergency towline was still stretching tight across the sky.

Silence, except for the racing hum of the engine, and the windy buffeting noise of air rushing past outside.

'We did it,' James began to say in wonder, just as the tow line reel made a going loose beginning to haul back in sound.

They waited, hearts on edge. It did it again, but only sounding like half a turn. The line was still tight. There was still something on the other end.

'We did! We did! We did!' squeaked James.

And both of us are still alive, Mark thought, looking at the back of James' head. The relief of that thought was better, a thousand thousand times better, than the excellent feeling during the most urgent pee. His thoughts ran on. They were screaming across the sky, so what was next? Yes, now we just have to land safely. Somewhere. How was he supposed to land the Happy Flier with a towline dangling something from the front? Now he thought of it, soon flying her would become impossible, once they were both travelling at the same speed, and the towline went slack. The Fly-ahead would begin to fall out of the sky, and they would have to follow. For as long as he could, he needed to be flying slower than the Fly-ahead. That couldn't last forever. Sooner or later, when the tow line reeled all the way in, the little space ship dragging in the air would be heaps worse than having the wheels on the Happy Flier down. They would crash out of the sky for sure. He slowed the engine a little, then a little more.

'It's not very the same,' James was saying.

'What?' he asked, coming out of his thoughts.

'It's not very the same as home down there,' said James.

It wasn't. It looked like huge waves of a sea, but it was dirty sand coloured. They were a long way from home, and going further away every second. While the Fly-ahead was in front there was no way of turning around. James was looking through the rest of the instruction pages. Now looking at his controls. Looking down at the pages again.

'Can we still be flying for one hour?'

In one hour? He had no way of working that out. He slowed the motor some more, to save fuel. The towline needed to stay tight anyway. He thought of the wing extensions. He put them back out so a gentle drag would happen. That felt better. The Happy Flier lifted a little, and felt like she weighed something in the sky again. Maybe she was big enough to carry the Fly-ahead. With the motor running flat out she might be. But he would need all the fuel for that. He stopped the motor altogether. It hummed, whirred, and then did a final little wiz sound. Silence in the sky again, with just the sound of the wind buffeting past the fuselage.

'You have to haul Cort back in with the tow reel, bit by bit, so the line stays tight. Why do we need one hour?' he said. James was turned around on his seat, looking up and back.

'We sound really grown up, don't we. One hour... It's not printed, it's scribble along the side, but Avro wrote the time an hour from now, and I think it says "hospital ship pumps into atmosphere?". Or maybe "jumps". He doesn't write very good for a grown up.'

'Yeah well... and how are they going to do anything anyway, if we're still crashing through the sky. We have to look after ourselves.'

'Do you know?' James asked, sounding unsure, 'do you know things to keep us good?'
Safe. He means safe thought Mark.

'No. We have to work things out for ourselves, while this is happening.'

'Oh.'
James was turning back around, sitting back down.
'Do I have to keep my harness on?'

'Yes.'
It was beautiful up here, and so quiet, just windy sounds rushing past. Nothing seemed to be changing, but every second they must be rushing closer to the land way down below. He looked again at the towline, as James was hauling it in another turn of the drum. It seemed to be angling slightly down into the sky ahead. His eyes followed it out into the distance. He could see something, a dark blob on the end. A sort of dirty ball shape.

'What if it's not him? What if we caught something else?' asked James into the silence, right when Mark was having the same thought.

What else could it be?

'It might be that rubbish bin thing with the mini ray gun on top… or, or the dual fighter?'

'That's not a dual fighter. Hey – I heard it anyway, the dual fighter. It landed last night.'

'Really?'

'Yep. In the really middle of the night. It made this sky ripping noise, and then went like "bang", real hard into the ground. A long way away but.'

'You didn't say,' said James looking around.

'You and Shane wouldn't wake up, and it only happened once, so there was nothing anyway, if you did.'

'Oh. We could have gone searching. It might have been really exciting!'

'No, it was far away, like further than… like far as this.'

'That's too far for us,' decided James, 'for going exploring I mean.'

No joking Mark thought sarcastically. Sometimes James had no idea. The towline was definitely angling down. Things were going to get bad soon. How would he get them both out of this?

'James, why didn't you go to the hangar like I said? Everything's going to go crap soon, and you shouldn't be here.'

'I have to be real sneaky sometimes, coz Alan tries to go places without me. I hate when I'm left behind. You were going to leave me behind. I just knew, and it made me feel really unhappy.'

'Yeah well, better unhappy than dead.'

Mark laughed at his next thought.

'You must be a total rat of a little brother sometimes.'

'Yeah,' said James, like he was thinking about it, 'Well I,' he began, sounding sooky, but then he lost interest, and changed the subject. 'It is the Fly-ahead, look, you can see like dull reflections off flatnesses of glass.'

The sun had gone over the horizon behind them, and everything was getting dusky, but he thought he could see what James was talking about.

'Why didn't you want me to come?' asked James, like it was something he had been putting off crying about.

'Because when the Fly-ahead slows down it's going to hang from the front of us, and drag us down until we crash, and then we will die, and that will hurt a lot, and I didn't want to feel bad about you as well as me, if things went bad.'

'Well… what if it isn't too heavy, and you fly us really good, and we can make it?'

'Umm…'

'Coz we're still going the wrong way? We could try now? Before the ground gets too close?'

Mark turned the ignition lever. The motor hummed into life again. He looked across the controls. Wing extensions were out to slow them down. He would leave them out for maximum lift. James was copying, looking along his controls with his fingers while he wound the towline in.

'What is "landing drag chute" do you reckon?' he asked.

'I don't know, but hey: don't look with your fing…'

It was too late. Just as James' fingers were feeling the knobby thing there was a bang, a roar from somewhere at the back of the Happy Flier, and they began to lose air speed.

'Sorry,' squeaked James.

'Sorry' just didn't cover it, Mark thought as he fought to control the slowing plane. It seemed the harder he ran the motor the less speed they had. The plane began to tilt. They were following the Fly-ahead down.

'Make it stop make it stop,' squealed James.

Tilting more, and more. A seat bolt came rattling down from way up the back, clattering as it bounced off things until it hit the back of his seat, hard. Bernard. Mark remembered Avro asking "Have you got all of them? Did you count them?". Bernard had said yes, but he was hopeless at counting. Tilting, tilting, and they were stopped still. The Happy Flier was hanging in the air, vertical, with the tow line hanging straight down. Now they were nose to the ground the motor was only making things worse. He turned it right down, to just an idling murmur. Chirping alarms and flashing red lights were all over his control console. The Happy Flier was telling him it couldn't fly on its nose. The desert was still a long way below, but they were going there, to crash in the middle of nowhere. That was the only way this could end. The Happy Flier was like a stick hanging in the air. He hung in his harness, none of him still touching the seat, looking out and down at the dirty sand ridges.

'It's very big!' said James. 'The motor is making it wobble.'
He looked to where James' head was turned, looking out the side window to up above them. A large square parachute, with a billowing bulge of air in it from where warm air from the motor was trying to rise and escape.

'Will the motor wreck it?' asked James concerned.

'No, coz I'll turn it off,' said Mark.
He did. There was a sinking feeling. This time he thought he really could see the sand ridges coming closer.

'On, on,' James was yelling.

'Okay! I'm doing it.'
Better. Floating in the sky like a hanging stick again, with the Fly-ahead below. Darkness was falling over everything.

'Wind up, wind up,' he said suddenly.
Was the fly-ahead boy all right? If he was, could they climb out and get him, then cut the space ship towline, so it fell, and the Happy Flier could fly again? No, of course they couldn't. It was minus forty-seven degrees outside, and the air was still too thin to breathe. Forty-seven degrees colder than when things turned to ice.

'Hey James? Stop. I have to think some more first.'
They were looking straight down into the little space ship.

'I can't see if he's all right,' said James, his voice unhappy, almost panicking.

'Lights... we need lights.'

Mark looked along the controls. There were three choices. Cabin? No, that made things worse. He heard James about to speak.

'Wait. Just wait, all right? I'm looking for the right switch.'

'Okay. You don't have to get bossy. I was just going to say the communicator hasn't worked yet, but it's blinking on a different number, like there's someone there.'

'Switch it then... no, <u>don't</u>,' yelled Mark.

He had just remembered who he was talking to; the 'switch everything to disaster' kid.

'Too late,' said James.

Nothing. No disaster, and then suddenly a voice. Mark listened, his hand hovering over the light switches.

'Recall the Fly-ahead. The planet arc channel is narrowing. Miss this return window and our six day trip becomes a four month long way home. We have eight minutes left. Anything needing rescuing will have to be handed to us on a plate now, or it's too late. Jam all frequencies and return to silent running. As far as this back end-of-nowhere world is concerned, we were never here.'

'Hello?' said James into the communicator.

No answer, and the light had gone out on the communicator box. There was no-one there. The hospital ship had come, and now it was collecting its own fly-ahead, and going home. There was nothing that could be done about that. He felt his heart sink, and then he returned his thoughts to what he was doing. Landing lights?

Click. Brilliant light everywhere, so sudden and bright that James screamed. Right below them was the fly-ahead boy, looking back. At least, his eyes were open. James was waving. The boy didn't wave back. He looked shrunken in his seat. His arm lifted, but then fell back above his shoulder, and stayed there. Gravity?

'It's too bright. The light's too bright. He's trying to shield his eyes,' said James, his voice sad with worry.

Worry that it wasn't true about the light being too bright, and that the truth was the fly-ahead boy's body was already dead, and just flopping around in the dangling space ship. Mark turned the landing lights off, and then clicked the other switch over. Navigation lights. Blue light, green light, red light, and a gentle yellow one, coming from different parts of the plane. They could still see the fly-ahead boy. He wasn't moving. James was turning around, looking to Mark.

'Help him,' he said, his voice breaking with tears.

'Shh. I can hear something. Something's going wrong with our plane.'

The sound was coming from… the back? No. From…? The sound was coming from everywhere.

'It sounds like the teachers on the staffroom microphone, when it comes out the playground speaker but we're too far away to hear,' said James.

'It is that sound,' decided Mark, 'but it's coming towards us. Something's going to hit us!'

They twisted around to look out the cockpit windows. Nothing. Now all of the Happy Flier was vibrating with the sound of the machinery of something very big coming close.

'Eeek!' squeaked James.

A bigger and bigger roundness like the nose of a huge ship was sliding underneath the dangling Fly-ahead.

'Land our Fly-ahead in the front cradle, then the craft to be rescued in the central hold down. We have one minute fifty-eight, fifty-seven, fifty-six. No mistakes, no holdups… …I have almost no register of body warmth, but there is the faintest steady heartbeat. Medivac, you will have to be quick, the quickest you've ever been. As soon as we have the landing bay sealed get the patient out of that mess, into a chamber and onto full life support. Don't waste time on diagnostics. One minute forty-one, forty, thirty-nine. Core temperature, heartbeat, breathing, brain pattern overlay, in that order. Thirty-six, thirty-five. All teams and equipment ready and in position.'

The hospital ship had HELP4U on it in big letters, not like a joke, but like an official number. There was a large open area inside its back. A Fly-ahead suddenly darted in from the dark and settled down onto a cradle at the front of the landing space. There was a girl inside. A girl with no helmet on, and two tails of hair. A girl like Joanne from space cadets. She waved up at James and Mark. She flicked off her harness and reached for her cockpit exit door control, but stopped like that, ready. She didn't open the glass lid. Outside her Fly-ahead, in the open landing bay, the thin air was still ice cold and unbreathable.

'I'm going to lower him?' said James.

'What? Sorry. I was thinking about space cadets,' said Mark quickly, 'Well go for it, fast as we can.'

'Me too about cadets – that's how I know to let the line out now,' said James.

The hospital ship was stationary below them, drifting with them through the dark sky. The damaged Fly-ahead was above another cradle like the one the girl had landed on. The drum in the Happy Flier turned as James worked the lever. Down went the little space craft. Grippers like big claws came out of the hospital ship's deck and took hold. Mark could see people in white waiting behind a glass door, some of them looking up at him. They were ready to come rushing out.

'We can't wait. We will lose the patient. Cut the cable get the roof closed and get in there now… Thirty seconds and we miss our path home. Twenty-five, twenty-four, twenty-three,'

A ray of light shot out from the side of the landing area, cutting the emergency tow line in a shower of sparks. In the Happy Flier the cable drum did a wild wiz noise, sucking the cut towline in like spaghetti. The other part of the tow cable fell onto the rescued Fly-ahead. Hatch covers were sliding across to meet in the middle over the hospital ship's landing bay. They shut. Now the top of the hospital ship was smooth. Things were happening inside, but James and Mark couldn't see or hear any of it. The hospital ship suddenly shot away out into the night.

GOING DOWN

'Umm,' said James.

They were alone, dangling from a large square parachute in a dark sky over a desert. They were a long way from anywhere.

'The bumheads didn't even say "hello",' said Mark.

'Or goodbye,' said James, 'but they rescued him. His heart is still working,' he added, like he was floating in a dream. They drifted quietly along in the sky, happiness for the fly-ahead boy filling their thoughts. The Happy Flier's motor hummed softly, lifting the chute above them with warm air.

'And who's going to rescue us?' asked Mark finally.

'We are?' suggested James.

He hung in his harness, looking at the readouts in front of him. They weren't really in front of him where they were supposed to be, they were below him, because the glider was still hanging vertical in the sky like a big hollow stick with wings. Wings that couldn't work while your nose was pointed straight at the land below. Just past the controls was the back of James' head, then the front cockpit window, and outside that a long drop in the dark to the desert sands. The desert; hard bits of rock and gritty dry sand that was waiting for the Happy Flier to reach it in a hull smashing wing tearing off crash that would kill him and James. There was no little screen in the controls where you could ask 'how can I rescue myself?'.

'Let's do it now,' said James, like they were playing a game.

Anger roared through him, anger at the childishness of James, at how young and trusting he was, at how pissweak little, and stupidly dangerous around switches, and…he realised James had turned around, to look up at him.

'Don't,' said James, his voice crying.

'Don't think bad things about me. I did have a plan. Not even a play one.'

'We need a plan right now,' Mark said back, ignoring the crying, 'so… tell it at me.'

'Well,' began James.

Even though he couldn't see it happening, he could tell James was winding his fingers up in knots, because he was shy about his plan being any good. Now James was doing that dark look he did, when he knew you were going to make fun of him. I won't, thought Mark, no matter how bad his idea is, because there's no

114

point. Why be nasty to someone for just being themselves, especially when you were about to die together.

'I saw it on Planetman.'

Now James was waiting, and frowning really bad at Mark. He was waiting for a Bernard and Philip type put down.

'And?'

'Oh… umm, he was like crashing, and then he pulled a lever and out came the 'mergency chute at the last second, and they were playing the "I won" music for the end, but it got tangled all up in itself and it wouldn't work, and Planetman goes, "I'm wishing I still wore nappies right now", and then he bangs his head on this lever with "pull me if the chute won't work" written next to it, and he's still crashing, but he can't make the lever move, because it's got like a safety clip, and then he gets that off, and like pulls the big lever, and "bang" the parachute thing is let go of, at the back of his ship, and the engine thing suddenly starts working again, and he goes flying safe across the sky, and,'

'Okay okay. You haven't breathed for like ages.'

'Do you like my plan?'

'If we can find a lever like that, to get rid of our parachute.'

'How about this one?'

'<u>NO</u>,' Mark yelled, but it was too late.

The chute unhooked from the tail above them with a sudden snap, and instantly they were falling, screaming down through the dark sky.

He had the controls in his hands, but they wouldn't do anything. James hadn't given him time to think, to get ready.

'Motor thing?' he heard James call out loudly, like it was just a suggestion.

As they fell, inside the Happy Flier sounded like the tearing of the sky he had heard in the middle of the night. Even the engine, as it rose to screaming as fast as it could, was hard to hear in the noise of the glider plummeting towards the land below.

Everything was shuddering and shaking, his harness, his seat, the cockpit windows, James' rooster tail of hair. Mark was straining at the controls. The desert was tilting, racing across in front of his eyes, faster and faster, closer and closer, flatter and flatter, and suddenly he was staring at the darkness of space, and stars, and feeling squashed back into his seat.

'Don't go too much?' called out James, as the Happy Flier began to shudder again.

They were going into a tail stall. He didn't have time to look at the readouts. He must be flying straight up into the sky nearly. It wouldn't come back over, the Happy Flier, even though he still had some air speed. Up and up, slower and slower...

'Are you doing a loop the loop Lefty?' James asked, like he expected Mark to do something extra, something surprising, to be funny.

I am he thought, but only because I have to. He remembered Avro's teaching, "No sudden changes. Adjust her slow and gentle, bit by bit". He eased the controls slowly over the opposite way, and the Happy Flier began to fall. As she lay over on her back, and he was hanging upside down in his harness again, he realised he didn't know how close below them the desert was. They were flying upside down now, he was sure of that much. Run the engine flat out and roll, roll her over he thought, determined to stay in control.

It felt more like doing a cartwheel in the school playground, and the Happy Flier came out of it flying skew-whiff across the sky, but now the desert was below, and the stars above. Everything was back how it should be. James was talking away happily.

'You know that thing, that stupid thing they say, about how you piss yourself if you're scared, well I didn't. It was like really good!'

Mark's heart was thumping fast, and so hard it hurt his chest. It was giving him a headache.

'We didn't even come close to crashing,' added James, turning around in his seat to look back at Mark.

'Yep. Good one,' said Mark, 'How about we figure out which way is home? Before we run out of fuel.'

'There's like really good stars, and I've got lollies?' said James.

So this was how grown ups felt – never getting to enjoy right now, always having to think and worry about what came next, for everyone to stay safe and happy. No, I'm not doing it Mark decided. It isn't my turn yet. It was the same as being brave. You were on duty all the time, every second of every day, and you never got to see how good, or exciting, or fun things were. I'm not doing it because I'm nearly ten, and I'm supposed to be learning and having fun. James was holding a packet of lollies out over the pilot controls, while he tried to understand the readouts upside down.

'Lolly,' he said, wriggling that hand in the air.
'How much is left? Fuel?'

'Don't know. It says an amount that's got four numbers in it, but I don't know how much goes for how long.'
Mark felt annoyed at himself that he didn't know. It was important. Mr Kopter would have known. Relax, he told himself – I'm a kid. Stay in this moment.

'Which way is home?' asked James, like it was a vaguely interesting idea to find out.
Mark just looked back, too tired to even bother answering.

They had used a lot of fuel getting high in the sky, trying to see a way home. The fuel readout had three noughts now, and only two numbers left. He wasn't letting himself panic, but he could feel it waiting, the hard scary worry, it was creeping up on him in the back of his thoughts. There was dull darkness below, a long way below: the desert, and everywhere else soft fuzzy dark blue night sky, full of stars.

'Turn off our lights?'
He didn't argue, just did it. James was out of his harness, nose pressed up against the glass.

'Now my eyes will work better, because I am being like a owl,' he said.
'I think I see something?' he added as he turned around.

'Play or real,' asked Mark.

'Hmm,' said James, just like Mr Arthurs did, when he meant 'go away, you are annoying me'.

In the starlight Mark could see James' eyes, like they were pools of still water. The black round bit in the middle had automatically gone really big to let more light in, so they would work better in the dark.

'Well?'

'Well what?' asked James back.

'Which way do I steer?'

'Me!?' asked James, like he couldn't believe it was up to him.

'Over there,' he said, sounding proud, and bashing his pointing arm into the cockpit window glass by accident.

'I think it's the Spaceport tower, you know the little light thing on the top.'

The chances were pretty good that it was the Spaceport tube tower. It was somewhere to aim for anyway. Slowly he began to bank the Happy Flier into a turn.

'We could glide? To save fuel? For in case I'm a bit wrong?'

'No. We can glide because it's a good idea, and the readout says there isn't much left,' Mark answered.

'Thanks,' said James, 'I found the way home didn't I. This is like my happiest day.'

It isn't mine, thought Mark, not yet. Not until we are safe, back on the ground.

COMING IN TO LAND

'And what's that one? That gauge there?'

'How high we are.'

'It's going down all the time. And that?'

'How fast. You better get in your own seat, because we could crash.'

'Okay. I'm still the lookout though, aren't I.'

Silence, except for the wind on the outside of the glider, and the click of James' safety harness catch. Gliding down through the sky. The desert below had changed to light patches that would be grass, with dark blobs that were probably trees. They were getting closer to home.

James was rabbiting on about things he liked.

'The Gorgelzoonies. I like them. I got undies for my birthday with them on the back. It's so when you fart they get to smell it first.'

They both chuckled, just guilty silly giggles. He and James understood it was small boy humour, but so what. He decided he didn't want to grow up before he had to.

'They're my favourite bad guys, coz they're so bad at it,' went on James.

'Yeah. They're so bad at being bad that they're good. They saved my life once.'

'Really?'

'Yep. That's how the scout pilot knew I was still there needing rescuing: the Gorgelzoonies ship out in space, turning into lots of coloured sparkly pieces.'

'Yeah... I wish you still had your Planetman. I want one for me more than anything.'

Me too, Mark thought. There was no thing he'd left behind on the old Family ship that he wanted more. Just the companionship of that small wiggly arms and legs spaceman. It wasn't going to happen. Not on this planet. Not for him. He knew he was lucky to have food for certain each day and a comfortable place to sleep. Expensive toys weren't going to happen. The closest any of them had come to having their own Planetman was Philip's cut out picture, and it wasn't the same anyway, not if he wasn't your own. You couldn't borrow a starter for your dreams.

'I did get one,' said James, beginning to talk again, 'Not a Planetman. An Alito. It doesn't do much, but you can't break it. I do like it a bit. It only says two things, and only when the weather changes. I dropped it down the back of the toilet once, and I forgot I did it, and then we couldn't find it anywhere. It wasn't until like the next Spring before he spoke. Mum was on the loo, and he suddenly goes "I'm Alito Magnificus. I'm the unbreakable child". She screeched. That was funny. Happy funny. I hope I never forget that. Hey? If it looks like the opposite of the Fly-ahead shadow, I mean like a light finger shape on the ground, could that be it? The runway? Just beyond those trees.'

He woke up with a jolt at the word 'trees'. He hadn't been paying attention to outside, because the Happy Flier had nearly been flying itself as it fell gently through the sky. He was sure it was the runway. They had fluked it almost right on course, but they were too low to be still in the air when they reached it, they needed to turn a bit, and where was the engine switch? One wing dipping down, the other pointing up into the night sky, turning, turning. His eyes were looking out into the darkness to level the plane, and down at the controls to find the starting lever. Everything was hard to see in the dark, inside and outside the plane, but if he turned on any lights he wouldn't be able to see anything for a moment, and every moment was important right now. Quick quick yes, please, engine… starting up. Spinning the revs up to flat out.

The Happy Flier surged forward with sickening speed and rose in the air like it had run into a rubbery cushion. At least it felt like that, but they were still falling towards the blank darkness of the ground below. Turn on the landing lights, now he'd done the engine? No, forget them, forget everything, concentrate on clearing those trees.

'Don't do the wheels!' squeaked James, 'not yet I mean.' There was a whipping hiss as the Happy Flier brushed over the treetops.

'I'm doing them I'm doing them,' yelled Mark, before James could start again about the wheels.

Before he even had time to worry about speed, or if the wings were level, or if the nose or tail were too low, the wheels clunked into place and hit the runway with a skidding squeal, and the Happy Flier was on solid ground again. He was crying and laughing, laughing and crying. It took two deep breaths and a couple more wonky giggles to get control of his feelings.

'Don't prang into Mr Kopter's fighter,' said James like a gentle warning.

There was a lot of runway to go yet. Down with the engine revs, out with the air brakes on the wings, ease on the wheel brakes to lose some speed, and now they were rolling along like a terrestrial car towards the hangar end of the airfield.

'I'm parking it right where it was,' said Mark, but in the dark he misjudged the big arc shape he had to turn, and they bumped across the airfield alongside the runway for a bit.

'Really close!' said James, leaning forwards in his seat as the Happy Flier became still.

He was looking out at the launching towline Mark had unclipped from the nose of the Happy Flier before they took off.

'We probably had enough fuel to do flying around, if you were scared about how quick we landed?'

Just as James was speaking the engine did a strange whirring rev, and spun down to silence.

'Nup,' said Mark, as he reached out and turned the engine switch to off.

All the blinking red lights that had just appeared went out. He felt his head come to rest on the control panel. He was so tired.

He woke up feeling better. Fresh. It was still dark. He could hear two noises, James doing little piggy snores, and something going slap, slap, slap. Now he knew where he was – in the Happy Flier. He grabbed at the controls in panic… no, he remembered landing safely. A hand appeared at the cockpit window, slap, and fell out of sight again. Someone was outside. He undid his harness and went to open the door out of the glider.

'You landed, and I runned all the way, and then you didn't come out! I've been banging the windows for ages!'

'We went to sleep.'

Shane was glowing excited.

'Well?'

'We… they came in a hospital ship and took him. He was still alive, a little bit.'

'Really? Really truly? Not playing?'

'Nup. It wasn't like playing. It was serious, and scary, and things kept going wrong, and we nearly died.'

'Oh… Sorry. You did rescue him! That is so amazing good! Hey – nobody knows you even went. They sent a trooper over to get us, for like a big lots of people dinner in the Base dining hall. If you sneak over there now you won't get in trouble for taking the plane?'

It did look the same where it was parked. Almost like it hadn't gone anywhere.

'Good idea!'

No, the wing extensions were still out, and there was no engine left to bring them in. I'm a kid: be in this moment, Mark told himself. Mr Kopter will understand, and anyway, tomorrow can be someone else's problem. The grown-ups can sort it out. Food, and something to drink, that's what he was interested in now.

They began walking over to the Base. There was James' parents' car. James went to it like a robot, opened the door, climbed in, and went to sleep again.

'He ate more lollies than me,' said Mark, meaning even if James didn't want any food, he would like to go and eat things.

They shut the door. Voices were coming from the Base entrance.

'I've looked everywhere. Haven't stopped looking since we got here. It would be those three. Damn silent little sneaks. Turn your back for two seconds and they're off. Why can't they think, you know, like a tiny little thought: will people be worried about me? Just once. Just one of them even.'

'I'm sure I saw your boy earlier. It's James that worries me the most. It's… he's… I'm not sure they know they need to look out for him, as well as for themselves.'

'There they are.'

Two dads and a man they didn't know were running towards them.

'Where's James? Lefty?' asked James' dad urgently.

Mark pointed into the car. Silence. Three grown ups just standing over them.

'You are good boys. We were a bit worried about you. Come and have some tucker. I saw orange drink in there. You like that don't you.'

Mark wanted to say he wasn't a baby, but, hey, he did like orange, and he'd like some right now.

'Yep,' he said, as they walked into the Deep Space listening outpost.

'Me too,' said Shane.

WAITING, HOPING, AND THE PAIN OF NOT BEING BELIEVED

A whole month went by. Every day Mark expected Mr Kopter to turn up at the school, to ask things about his plane. The emptiness of fuel, the missing half of the emergency tow cable, the sick all down the back of James' seat. And Mr Arthurs, why didn't he say one day whether the fly-ahead boy had got better? And Miss Shandy – they'd all tried to tell her about the rescue, but she just folded her smile away and looked like she wished they wouldn't. It was a mid-week day at school. It felt ordinary. They were sitting on the grass in the playground. James had a new planetman to show, but like Philip pointed out, it wasn't really new, just an old one of Alan's that their dad had cleaned up a bit and found a box for.

'They're doing their best,' said Shane, meaning the grown-ups, with his voice sounding like their best would never be good enough.

'I still like him,' said James, flying Planetman around in a circle in the air.

'A lot. I don't ever get anything that is just for me new, but I don't mind.'

'Hey, that Cort, that fly-ahead boy, well I wanted him to get saved as much as anybody, but making stuff up doesn't save someone, not when it's too late already,' said Philip.

This again thought Mark. It wasn't worth saying anything back.

'You know why you can't get away with that rescue story crap?' said Philip, 'They found it. The Fly-ahead. A big hole in the desert, with bits of it at the bottom all burned up and mangled. So no way you rescued that guy, and, if a hospital ship did come, the Spaceport tower would know all about it. So you're all bullshit. My dad said boys should keep their made-up stories where they belong – in the playground, and if he was your dad he would smack your bums until you apologised to everyone, for spruiking crap at them.'

'Yeah?' said Shane, 'Well my dad said don't listen to people who get their kicks out of being nasty, and I should be there for my friends when they need me.'

'Hey, I'm here aren't I? I was just saying,' said Philip, 'So no need to go all serious. Dad said did I believe it, and I said yes, I always believe Lefty and James, because they're my friends, and he said "Yeah well, Phil The Dill, who needs dickheads for friends?". I really hated him right then. I said you were more fun than him, and he was the dickhead, and then he slapped me one, and took my cadet club money back off me. Mum give it me again though.'

Bernard came running, looking pleased and excited.

'You lot are like so dead. Someone stole a big parachute thing from the airfield, and the police think it's you. You three. Cool hey. About time the goody goodies copped it. The two Goody Goodies and Lefty I mean. '

They ran with him to the listening position underneath the front office window.

'They reckon your fingerprints are like all over everything. They've got this map thing of the front window of the plane, with Shane written all over it, and arrows pointing to hand shapes. And they've got lots of other stuff.'

'Shush. We can't hear.'

Mr Arthurs was in there, and he was angry, in a hard-voiced way they had never heard before.

'NO. You are not going near my children. Use your brains; that parachute is too big to fit in a car, too heavy folded up with all its ropes for a grown man to drag, and these boys are nine and ten years old: light flimsy little things that can't even string three thoughts together in their happy empty little heads. Are you listening?'

'You aren't my teacher Arthurs, and you never were. We have evidence here that proves "your boys" are nasty mean-spirited thieves, who need unpleasant discipline to right their ways. Not happy with stealing, they vomited all over someone else's property. I bet they thought that was so funny.'

'I doubt it.'

'Doubt all you like. It had been cleaned up, but we found the evidence. I will say to you what I said to Kopter earlier: no point making excuses for them, or trying to shield the brats: evidence is evidence, and they have a lesson to learn. And while we're on the subject of unpleasant, your school is a dump, and I thank the stars my parents could afford better. Hand the boys over now or you will be charged with obstructing an officer in his lawful duty. Miz Anderson is here as my witness.'

'Sorry John, but I must do the right thing. I have my position to think of.'

'Shut up you stupid stupid people! I will not have you poisoning the boys' thoughts of themselves with these ridiculous accusations. Look at this: eighty-six litres of fuel siphoned. I can't even begin to understand how you can believe what you've written.'

Silence. The boys looked at each other. What was going to come next?

'Facts are facts. Theirs are the only fingerprints, and their grubby little mitts have been everywhere, all over everything. If you are too weak to face the facts, we will wait for someone to make you. I've called someone senior enough to put you in your place Arthurs.'

'Well thank you for that. I hope they have more than half a brain. I am expecting this community's Guardians of Childhood to arrive any minute, and I can assure you they will find your actions unacceptable.'

'Good.'

'Good yourself.'

James giggled softly.

'They are behaving like us, before we get a big telling off.'

'And here it comes,' said Bernard, but it was only Miss Shandy and Avro Kopter going in the school front doors.

'Uh oh,' said Shane, 'Look who's coming. It's your library man, and I think he's seen us.'

'Wow! Look at the size of that car. Is he trying to be like Master of the Universe or something.'

'Planetman – the enemy,' said James, facing Planetman so he could see.

They hurried, crouched down, around the side of the building.

'I bet he's gone inside by now?' said Mark.

He stuck his head around the corner to look. No-one there. They began creeping back to their listening post. The adult voices began again.

'Everybody's here. Good. Before you all start, things have changed. Does anyone mind if I close this? There are a few pairs of ears outside.'

The window slid shut.

'Bumheads,' said Bernard, 'we should get to know – it's about us.'

'He was carrying stuff,' said Philip.

'Handcuffs for you three,' joked Bernard, 'Lefty, I thought your "super amazing rescue" story was the best, it had them all going really weird cranky, the way you wouldn't give it up. This is the most ace thing you've ever done. Had me sucked in even.'

'They weren't handcuffs,' said Shane.

'No, it was like a fancy picture with writing, and a box.'

'And he didn't look cunning angry?' added James.

'Nearly sounded human for once,' agreed Shane.

They went back to sit on the grass in the playground. Bernard was still excited, like they were all in the middle of a big adventure.

'The policeman kept saying, when I was at the window the first time, he kept saying "that Left child and his little friend". That means you. You two. You are so dead. So dead.'

'You said that already,' said Shane.

There were grown-up voices in the distance.

'I can do it. No need for a crowd.'

They looked at each other.

'Do what?' said Shane, while their ears strained for more. They heard a door shut, or open, and then more talk.

'All right! I hear you. I won't be making a speech, or giving a lecture. I am well aware this is not about me.'

Mark saw Library man first, coming towards them past the only decent big tree in the playground. Why run? Where to even? He drew a one person going home rocket in the dirt with a stick instead. A shadow fell across his drawing.

'Boys, I have something for you here. A reconstructed solid materials matrix message that came to my office. A plaque, here it is, it has a picture of you two flying a plane, and it says "To the crew of the Happy Flier, for a rescue so flawless it will remain forever in our thoughts, and our hearts. Well done", that's from the crew of a hospital ship from Terra called the HELP4U.'

Mark could see it wasn't him and James flying, it was him and James in the Happy Flier's cockpit, hanging in the air above the hospital ship's upper deck. Library man was placing the picture down on the tufts of grass.

'Also there is this. Your teachers and I didn't open it, in case it only works once.'

Mark looked up. It was a hologram message toy. A small box that a moving 3D image would come out of.

'Everyone ready? Here we go then.'

The fly-ahead boy appeared, a shimmering light statue of him. Almost half as big as a real boy. There was the bit missing from the middle of his eyebrow, where the purple ray had got him. He was in a new flying suit, holding his space helmet in one hand. His head kept moving slightly forwards and back while he repeated some words. He really meant whatever he was saying, but the sound from the box was a bit far-away soft. They all leant in to listen.

'Thank you. Thank you. Thank you?'

'That's all I have to say to you too,' said the man, from where he was crouched down next to them.

'Thankyou. To all of you boys, and especially to you Mark, and you, James.'

The man walked away across the playground.

James pressed the stop button by accident while he was feeling it. The fly-ahead boy vanished. Just the sound of other children playing now, yelling, jumping, chasing, in the playground around them. It was all over.

Mark felt like he wasn't ready. Not yet. There should be more? His heart hurt because he just knew there should be more. After such a big adventure, how could it end with nothing, just a sitting around together in the sandy dirt of a school playground?

'That's a daylight charging panel, that grey bit,' said Bernard, like he was explaining something.

'So what?' said Philip.

'I'm just saying – it's like meant to go lots of times, it could go forever.'

James pressed the button again, and there was Cort looking at them, and saying "thank you, thank you, thank you?". James was holding him out for Mark to take. It was easy to see it was hurting James a lot, but James was determined to be fair. That was more important.

'He gets even less good things than me,' James said, not looking at anyone.

Mark could feel Shane's eyes. Serious eyes.

'You have it,' he said to James.

'Really?'

'Yep.'

He had never seen James so happy. Not 'forever in this moment happy' like this. As Mark looked at the statue, at James, at Shane, and at the rest of the cadet club gang sitting around on the grass, a beautiful feeling flooded his heart, and his thoughts. A tangy sadness followed by a feeling of things being complete, a knowing that in the end everything, at this moment, had finally gone right.

James was poking something at him. A little man in a box.

'Yours now,' James said.

He knew he couldn't take it. James was still holding it out.

'It's for keeps, so you don't have to be alone in space when you go to find your family.'

They were all looking at him, like this was something they'd known about him for a long time – that he would go, and he would be lonely.

'We're writing all our names on the box?' asked Shane.

'Yeah,' said Bernard, handing over a pen.

'Can I? Coz I wasn't even there, not that day,' said Dennis.

'Everyone,' insisted Shane.

'You never get a birthday Lefty. Nobody knows when to,' said Philip, as he wrote his name as tidy as he could.

'Yeah,' said Bernard, 'today can be Lefty's birthday. We'll pool our tuckshop money.'

'I never forget you gave me that coin back,' said James as he handed Planetman over, 'it was for my first night of cadet club. That meant everything to me.'

Mark hugged Planetman to his heart, and brushed away the tears trying to leak from his eyes. There would be more bad times, but from now on good things were going to happen too. He had the whole Universe to explore, and when he woke up tomorrow, he would be at the start of the rest of his life.

A kid was standing on top of a rubbish bin, and yelling "I'm Alito Magnificus, King of Everything". No you're not thought Mark, remembering Mrs Benson's story when he first arrived on Outer 17, because Alito Magnificus isn't King of Everything, he is the Unbreakable Child, and if he is real, he is the same as my family – somewhere out there in the hugeness of space, needing to be found.

The End